W9-CUJ-046

The Life of a Cowboy

Stu Campbell

Copyright © 2018 by Stu Campbell

All rights reserved. No part of this book may be reproduced or utilized in any form or by any means, electronic or mechanical, including photocopying, recording, or by any information storage and retrieval system, without permission in writing from the author, except for review purposes.

This is a work of fiction.

ISBN: 978-0-9988499-3-5

6   5   4   3   2

Edited by Mira Perrizo
Cover and text design by D.K. Luraas
Cover painting by R. Loren Schmidt

Printed in the United States of America

1

The morning was cold and wet. The horse was shivering as I put the nosebag on him. I hoped the grain would warm him up. I hobbled him and went to the barn to get the curry comb and brush. I needed to get the snow off him before I saddled him.

I figured between eight inches and a foot of snow had fallen during the night. It was hard to tell. The wind had blown the snow into large snowdrifts against the barn and corral posts. I had to kick snow away from the barn door before I could open it. I didn't really want one, but I wished I had a shovel. I was glad I'd bought some cowboy boot overshoes, at least my feet would stay dry. Cold, but dry. I was wishing I'd have bought boots a couple of sizes larger. Then I could have put on an extra pair of socks to help keep my feet warm.

I brushed the snow off the horse. His back was still wet, but I couldn't completely dry him off. I went back to the barn, put the brush and curry comb away and got the saddle pad and blankets. The pad and blankets were stiff from the cold and I folded them a couple of times to try and get them loosened up. With the pad and blankets under my arm, I grabbed my saddle and went back outside.

The cold wind made me catch my breath for a second when I left the barn. The barn offered some protection from the wind, although it was cold inside. I put my head down against the wind and went to the horse. I was glad I had a scotch cap on, it had earmuffs! It would have been difficult to keep my cowboy hat on in this wind.

I put the pad and saddle blankets on the horse's back and, holding them in place with my left hand, threw my saddle on his back with my right hand. I moved it around to get it positioned in the right place, then walked around to the off side of the horse to undo the cinch from the cinch holder. I went back to the near side of the horse and reached under him to get the cinch. I put the latigo through the cinch ring and as I slowly tightened the cinch, I could see the horse tense up. He developed a small hump in his back and I figured he'd probably buck when I stepped on him, if he'd let me.

I tightened the cinch a little more, just enough to keep the saddle in place, and took off the hobbles. The horse stepped away, but didn't come unglued. I led him around for a few minutes then took the slack out of the cinch. I had the cinch tight enough that I could keep the saddle in place, but walked the horse around some more. I wanted to be as sure as I could that the horse wouldn't buck, but as cold as it was, I couldn't be sure of anything. I knew it would be a little difficult getting on the horse with my long johns, Levis, and shotgun chaps on. It wasn't anything new, I'd been doing it all winter, but the extra clothing restricted my freedom of movement. I really appreciated the summer when I wore my "chinks" and had more freedom to get on and off a horse.

I put a hackamore on the horse. I really didn't like using a bit and bridle on a horse during the cold winter months. Often, a steel bit would freeze to the edges of a horse's mouth and cause him a lot of discomfort.

After I'd walked the horse around about ten minutes to untrack him, he seemed to relax. *I guess I'd better get on him,* I told myself. I looked around the corral and half-jokingly thought, *All this fresh snow will make for a softer, although cold, landin' if he does throw me off!*

I checked the cinch again. With my left hand, I took hold of the headstall on the hackamore, cheeking the horse, and with my right hand I took the stirrup, turned it toward me and started to get on. The horse pulled away from me as I put my foot in the stirrup, making my foot slip out of the stirrup.

"Well, ol' man," I said, "we're goin' to do this as often as we have to until I get on! It would be most helpful if you'd cooperate!"

I went through the same procedure again, cheeking the horse. This time, my foot slid out of the stirrup when I put it in. The soles of my over boots had become slick with packed snow.

"Perhaps," I told the horse, "it would be helpful if I were a little more agile gettin' on!"

Again I repeated the procedure and got in the saddle. It wasn't the most graceful mount I'd ever done, my foot was slipping out of the stirrup as I sat in the saddle, but I was horseback. The seat of the saddle sure was cold!

I sat still in the saddle for a minute, surprised that the horse hadn't bucked or pulled away at my clumsy mount. I shifted my weight in the saddle and straightened it. I'd pulled it over a little getting on.

Gingerly, I touched the horse with my spurs, expecting the horse to come unglued. The rowels on my spurs were frozen and I had the thought that touching him with a spur might be just like stabbing him with a short knife!

Hesitantly, the horse stepped forward. Squeezing my legs against his sides, I urged him on. He took short, choppy steps. He seemed like he didn't want to move in this cold weather. I didn't have a tight rein on him, the horse was free to do what he wanted.

I urged him on some more. All of the sudden, he bogged his head and took a big jump forward. He didn't catch me totally by surprise, but he loosened me in the saddle. I tried to pull his head up with both hands on the mecate, but couldn't do it, he was too strong for me.

His second jump loosened me more in the saddle. I kept trying to pull his head up with my left hand. With my right hand I was pulling on the saddle horn, trying to stay in the saddle. My gloves were wet and my hand kept slipping off the horn. In the middle of his second jump, he kicked his hind feet out, pushing me forward in the saddle. By doing so, the horse helped me regain my seat and balance in the saddle.

It's strange what I remember when I'm in the middle of an unexpected event. I remember seeing the horse's breath as he exhaled and seeing the corral fence. I remember thinking, *If he hits the fence, he'll go down!* I even had the quick, momentary thought, *Maybe I should bail off!* While I was doing all this thinking, I was also trying to stay on as best I could.

When the horse hit the ground again, he ducked to the left. I could feel myself slipping off to the right. With a desperate, almost super human effort, I grasped the horn with my right hand and pulled myself back into the saddle. I was also pulling on the mecate with my left hand with all my strength. The horse went over on his right side. I don't know if I pulled the horse over, or if he slipped on the slick snow, but he was down on his side and I was still on him, somewhat.

As I felt him going down, I instinctively freed my right foot from the stirrup and put it down out away from the horse on the ground. The horse hit the ground on his right side, but my leg wasn't under the horse. I'd possibly saved myself a broken leg by doing so.

The horse laid there on the ground. I had his head pulled back to the left as far as I could so he couldn't get up. I held him down until he stopped fighting.

"I'll let you up when you've decided to cut out this monkey business," I said. "It won't hurt you at all to lie here and think about what you've done!"

As I sat kinda in the saddle and kinda off it, I thought, *I ought to get my left foot out of the stirrup. When I let him up, if I fall off, it might not be so good to get hung up in the stirrup!*

I pulled my foot from the stirrup and when I did, I scraped his side with my spur. He kicked and struggled, but I kept him down. I was sitting on him and thinking I could get off right here. But then I thought, *I'd just have to get back on him. I better stay here and try to stay on when I let him up.*

In my mind's eye, I was trying to picture how a horse got up. Does he get up with his hind feet first or his front feet? I couldn't remember. Then I pictured a cow getting up. A cow gets up with her hind feet first then her front feet. A horse gets his front feet under him first, then gets his hind feet under him.

I prepared myself for a sudden lurch from the front end of the horse as I gave him his head.

The horse was free to lie there and he did just that for a minute. I slapped him on the neck to encourage him and felt his front legs stretch out in front of him.

"Here goes!" I said to the horse.

I felt him raise up in front and righted myself in the saddle. I didn't have either foot in either one of the stirrups, but decided to let the horse up anyway. I prepared myself for the sudden lurch when he got his hind legs under him and got up. I knew it would push me forward and prepared myself as good as I could.

The horse got up and I felt clumsy as I was rocked back and forth. But I was still in the saddle! I fished with my feet for the stirrups and found them. I let the horse stand for a minute, then touched him, gingerly, with a spur and asked him to move forward.

The horse walked out, hesitantly. I walked him around in the corral until I felt him relax. Then I urged him into a trot. He moved out freely. I trotted him in the corral until I felt like he'd settled down.

"Now it's time to go to work," I told the horse. The whole process of getting the horse saddled and getting the kinks out of him had taken half an hour, maybe forty-five minutes. It didn't make any difference, I wasn't working on the clock. The sun had just come up when I started and I couldn't tell from the sun how long I'd been. There wouldn't be much sun, as the low-hanging clouds blocked it. I couldn't tell if it was going to snow more or just stay cloudy all day.

I opened the gate from horseback and rode out of the corral. I was hoping there wouldn't be much work today. I'd worked up a sweat trying to control the horse and started to take a chill. It was cold.

My job was to watch after a bunch of cows as they calved. It was late February and a few of the cows had already calved out. The cows were expected to really start calving around the first of March. There was an old set of corrals and a run-down shed where I could put those cows that looked like they were going to calve soon. The shed didn't offer much protection from the elements, a windbreak was about all that it provided, but it would be helpful to the newborn calves in inclement weather.

I hadn't put any cows in the corral that needed checking. I was riding the creek bottom, looking for cows that might have calved during the night. The willows were covered with snow and as I rode through them, the snow brushed against my chaps and coat. In a lot of places, I had to duck my head to get under the snow-laden branches. I was getting real wet, real fast.

I rode for about an hour without seeing any newborn calves and was ready to head back to the barn when I spotted a cow with a newborn calf. The calf was up and sucking, but shivering. It was cold. The cow had already cleaned the calf off.

I thought that I'd better take them back to the shed. At least the calf would get some protection from the wind there. I started toward them, but then stopped. I'd decided that the milk that the calf was getting from the cow would do more to help the calf warm up than the shed. I waited until the calf stopped sucking, then moved them toward the shed.

The calf was still unsteady on his feet, just learning how to walk and it was slow going. The calf was having a hard time following in the footsteps of his mother in the fresh snow. At one point he laid down. I decided to get off my horse and get the calf up. I couldn't just leave them out in the snow. And, I thought that walking might warm up my feet.

As I approached the calf, the cow turned on me. I had to position myself so that the horse was between me and the cow. That was difficult in the fresh snow, but I managed. The cow stopped before she hit the horse and turned back to her calf. She didn't know I was trying to help her and the calf.

Now I had a predicament. I really needed to put the calf on the horse, get on the horse and have the cow follow us to the barn. But I wasn't sure I could get back on the horse with the calf already on him and with the stirrups icy and slick. But I had to try. And I wasn't sure the cow would let me catch the calf.

I considered my options. I could rope the cow, tie her to a tree, get the calf on the horse and take him back to the barn, then come back and get the cow. Or, I could continue to follow the pair and drive them to the barn. To rope the cow, I had to get back on the horse and I wasn't sure I could do that with the buildup of ice on the stirrups and the bottom of my feet.

I decided to follow the pair to the barn. If I roped the cow and tied her to a tree, she'd choke herself and die before I could get back to her. I wasn't sure I could get back on the horse with the calf. Following the pair to the barn was the best option, although it would take the better part of the morning.

I followed the calf, keeping an eye on the cow. We made progress, although it was slow. I wasn't walking fast enough to get my feet warm and was really looking forward to getting to the barn. I'd put the cow and calf in the shed, put the horse in the barn, and then go to the bunkhouse and get warm myself. But at the rate we were going, it would be quite a while. I didn't look forward to remaining out in the cold for long.

We got to within a hundred yards of the shed and the calf fell again. He was just learning how to walk and I was speeding up the process. I decided to carry the calf the last hundred yards. I figured he only weighed about fifty or sixty pounds. The shed and barn looked inviting. There was some protection from the wind inside and the sooner I got them and the horse inside, the sooner I could go to the bunkhouse and get myself warm.

The last hundred yards were difficult. The calf struggled and squirmed all the way as I carried him to the shed. I suppose, even at his young age, just a few hours old, he didn't like to be manhandled. And he seemed to get heavier as I carried him. We finally made it to the corrals and the shed.

I carried the calf into the shed and put it

down. My arms ached as I released the calf. The cow followed me into the corral and went to the calf and started licking him. I was glad to see that. At least the cow wouldn't reject the calf. I threw the cow some hay and took the horse to the barn.

I put a nosebag of grain on the horse. As I unsaddled him, I said, "There wasn't much sense in saddlin' you this morning an' goin' through all the monkey business we did. I spent most of the mornin' afoot with that calf!"

I took off the nosebag, threw the horse some hay and went to the bunkhouse. The bunkhouse was cold. The fire in the stove had burned out and I got it going again. As the unused coffee heated up, I warmed my hands by the fire. My feet were still cold and I stomped them on the floor to warm them up. My hands were too cold to take off my overshoes.

The bunkhouse was fairly primitive. There was a cook stove, a pot-bellied stove, a table and chairs, and two bunk beds. There was no electricity but there was a battery-operated clock on one wall. Light was provided from a kerosene lantern. There was a hand pump for water over the sink.

Before I took off my chaps, overshoes and

boots I thought, *I'd better bring in plenty of wood and let it dry off.* It was my intention to stay inside the rest of the day and stay warm and dry. My chaps were wet and my pants were wet above where I'd had them tucked inside my over boots. My coat was soaked on the outside, but still dry on the inside.

I went outside, brushed the snow off the wood I intended to bring inside and brought in enough to keep the fire going for three or four days. The cook stove and a pot-bellied stove were all I had to keep the place warm. By the time I'd brought in the wood, the fire in the cook stove was going good. The coffee had heated up, so I poured myself a cup and took off my coat. I hung it on a chair and put the chair in front of the stove so the coat would dry off. Then I took off my over boots and boots. In between sips of coffee, I took off my wet clothes. My jeans were soaked clear through to my long johns.

2

There I was, butt naked from the waist down when the door opened up. I was surprised! It was Phil, the owner of the ranch. He had a big sack in one arm.

"This is a heck of a time to start a nudist colony!" he said, as he surveyed my situation. He set the sack on the table.

"I ain't startin' a nudist colony," I said, as I pulled on some dry long johns. "I got plenty wet bringin' in a newborn calf this mornin' an' need to dry off. There's coffee on the stove, help yourself. This is a heck of a time to come visitin'."

"I brought you some groceries. There's more in the truck."

"I wished I'd have known you were comin', I'd have waited to change out of the wet clothes," I said, as I pulled on a pair of dry jeans.

"No need for you to come out. There's only one more sack. I'll get it," said Phil. "No sense in you getting wet all over again."

Phil went to get the other groceries and I started the fire in the pot-bellied stove. I hung my wet jeans and long johns on a chair and placed it so they would dry in front of the stove. I pulled my boots on and was dressed again.

"You brought in a newborn?" asked Phil.

"Yep," I replied.

"It's a little early to start calving."

"There's usually a few early arrivals," I said. "The cold weather might have somethin' to do with it. Seems like miserable weather always has somethin' to do with cows calvin'. That ol' horse you gave me sure don't like to be saddled an' rode on a cold mornin'."

"Did he give you some trouble?"

"Quite a bit," I replied. "I almost pulled out my saddle horn just tryin' to stay on him!"

"He's not an old horse, only about six or seven. But he did buck pretty good when I broke him. Maybe he just don't like the cold weather."

"He ain't the only one," I said.

"Do you want another horse?" asked Phil.

"No," I replied. "I've put plenty of miles on

him already an' he only humped up a little. This mornin' was the first time he really bucked. He just needs more ridin'. He'll be all right."

"I'll bring you another one anyway. You'll need another one when the calving really starts. Right now, we're about two weeks or so away. I'll bring one out when the weather clears up. I was in four-wheel drive all the way here this morning. Do you want a colt? The best time to break a horse is when you're calving."

"I'd take a colt, if he was already started," I said.

Phil and I visited for another hour or so, then he made ready to leave. Before he left, he said, "Just sit out this storm. It's supposed to last another two, maybe three days. When it quits, it's supposed to warm up."

I asked, "Why don't you feed?"

"We haven't fed anything for about twelve or fifteen years. The cattle winter down here and there's always been plenty of feed out here on this desert. That's what makes this ranch ideal. We do grow some hay, but generally only feed the saddle horses at the main ranch. We bring some up here to feed a few horses. There's a stack of hay about a mile long farther south. It's been there a long time and the one end has turned black. It's no good. We put a little down there every year, just for emergency use."

"Don't you think this is an emergency now?" I asked.

"Not yet," said Phil. "This is supposed to blow over soon and the cattle can find plenty of feed on the ridgetops. The wind clears the feed up there."

"I'd think those cattle would need more feed when they're fixin' to calve," I said. "I'll still check those cows. I don't want to lose any calves. If I'm not mistaken, that's what you hired me for."

"Suit yourself, I'll be back in about two weeks," said Phil as he headed to the door. "Stay warm!"

"You bet!"

I followed Phil to the door and watched him get in his truck and drive away.

I looked at the clock on the wall. It was past three o'clock in the afternoon. We'd spent more time visiting than I'd figured. I thought that Phil didn't want to leave the warm bunkhouse and I didn't blame him.

I started some supper and while it heated up, I bundled up and went outside and fed the horse and cow. The cow's calf was up and sucking and that was a good sign.

After I ate, I cleaned the dishes using the water from the hand pump over the sink. I read some old magazines that were in the bunkhouse. I'd read through all of them before and wished I'd asked Phil to bring me some new, current reading material. Before I went to bed, I filled up the pot-bellied stove so that the fire would burn most of the night. I figured I'd have to get up around two or three o'clock to get the fire going again, and didn't look forward to it. I went to bed fairly early.

The next morning I got up, got dressed real fast, stoked the coals in the pot-bellied stove, started a fire in the cook stove and got coffee started. I warmed myself by the fire as the coffee began to boil. I thought that by keeping the fire going all night, it kept the water that came from the hand pump from freezing.

When the coffee was ready, I poured a cup and sat down between the two stoves. I felt fairly comfortable, as I had heat coming from both sides. I looked out the window and couldn't see much. The window was covered with ice. There weren't any curtains on the window.

Warmed up sufficiently, I went to the door, opened it and looked outside. I was greeted with a blast of cold air and cold, wet snowflakes hit my face. It was still snowing and the wind was blowing hard. Quickly, I surveyed the situation, and rapidly closed the door. I thought that there was about six or eight inches of new snow.

"Another cup or two of coffee won't hurt," I said to myself out loud. I talked to myself quite a bit when I was alone. It broke the monotony. When with others, I didn't talk much. I was content to listen and generally only made comments when directly spoken to.

Still talking to myself, I said, "Maybe it will warm up some an' the wind will die down when it's time to go out. I don't look forward to it! I wonder what that ol' horse will do this mornin'."

Another cup of coffee by the fire seemed to be the most prudent thing to do. I checked the clock. It was quarter after seven. I had plenty of time to do nothing other than stay warm.

At nine o'clock and after numerous trips to the outhouse due to the coffee, I bundled up and went outside. My chaps had dried overnight.

"What are you goin' to do this mornin'?" I asked the horse as I slipped a nosebag of grain on him. I put the hobbles on him and asked, "Did you learn your lesson yesterday? I hope so. It's too cold to mess around with that monkey business you did yesterday. What do you think of these banker's hours we're keepin' now?"

I brushed off the snow from the horse's back. There wasn't much. The horse's own body heat had melted a lot of it.

I got the saddle blankets and pad. They were stiff, frozen. I folded them a time or two trying to get them to loosen up. I thought, *Maybe I ought to take the blankets an' pad in the bunkhouse at night. At least they wouldn't be frozen.*

I got the saddle and went to saddle the horse. He humped up a little as I drew the cinch tight.

"Ah, ha!" I said. "A repeat of yesterday! Well, we'll just warm you up a little more today before I get on."

The horse had finished his grain and I took the nosebag off. I put the hackamore on and took off the hobbles. I started the horse walking around me, holding onto the long end of the mecate. Soon I had him trotting in a circle around me. I had him going around to the left and kept him going for about ten minutes. Then I started him going around to the right.

When he started to the right, he bucked a couple of jumps and I let him. "Go ahead, get it out of your system!" I told him.

I had him circle around to the right for another

ten minutes, then checked the cinch and made ready to get on. I tucked the long end of the mecate in my belt, cheeked the horse, put my foot in the stirrup and swung into the saddle. I felt kinda clumsy as I swung into the saddle. It wasn't as smooth as I would have liked, but I had too many clothes on to be graceful.

I was in the saddle. I just sat there for a minute, adjusting the saddle on the horse's back. The horse didn't do anything. I touched him softly with a spur and the horse hesitantly took a step forward. The horse acted like he didn't know whether he wanted to buck or just walk out. I urged him again with a spur and he walked forward.

"That's it," I said. "Just walk. Slow an' easy to start with." We walked around the corral for a few minutes then went to the gate, opened it and went out. I rode by the shed where I'd put the cow and her calf in yesterday. The cow hadn't cleaned up the hay I'd thrown her and I figured she had enough to keep her during the day.

We left the corrals and started out to look for cows. I didn't ride through the willows along the creek as I'd done yesterday. I thought if I stayed out in the open, I'd stay drier. And I could still look into the creek bottom for cattle. I had to ride quite a way before I saw any cattle. They had drifted with the storm and were a long way from where they should be.

When I finally found cows, I checked through them and didn't see anything that looked like it was going to calve any time soon. I had a number of marker cows, cattle that were of a different color or had distinct markings, and found all of them. I was satisfied that I'd seen most of the cattle.

I turned back toward the cabin and into a cold wind. I figured it was well past dinnertime and it would be closer to suppertime when I got back. The wind was cold and my horse didn't want to head into it. I didn't like the wind either, but it was the only way home. I urged the horse into a trot. The sooner we got home, the sooner we'd be warm.

We made it to the barn. I grained the horse as I unsaddled him and threw the cow enough hay to keep her overnight. The calf was up and actually running around. "If you'd have done that when I brought you in here, I wouldn't have had to walk so far," I said.

I went back to the horse, took off the nose-bag, threw him some hay and went to the cabin. It was cold inside and I got a fire going in the cook stove real fast. As the leftover coffee from the morning heated up, I got the fire going in the pot-bellied stove. I checked the clock. It was past four o'clock. Time for supper.

I took my time taking off my winter clothing and chaps. As the room warmed up, I'd take off another layer, in between sips of hot coffee. Soon I was warm and ready to start supper.

I followed the same procedure the next two days, seeing fewer cows each day. On the third day, I opened the door of the cabin and saw the sun. The storm had passed, but it was still cold. The air was filled with crystals that appeared to be little diamonds. They sparkled and shined in the sunshine. I never have figured out the reasons for this occurrence in nature, I think it has something to do with the amount of moisture in the air and the temperature.

I started toward the barn to saddle the horse when I heard a truck struggling through the snow. I waited until the truck made it into the yard to see who it was and what they wanted. It was Phil and he had a snowplow on the front of the truck.

"You got any coffee left?" he asked as he got out of the truck.

"Yep," I answered, "an' it's still hot."

I turned to go back into the bunkhouse and Phil followed. "What's up?" I asked, as I poured a cup for Phil. "It seems like the couple of weeks until you said you were goin' to show up have passed kinda fast. Either that or I've overslept."

Phil grinned. "No. I've come out to help you move."

"Move?" I questioned. "Has the landlord raised the rent?"

Phil grinned again. "I'm the landlord and I ain't made a cent in rent. But the main herd has drifted with the storm and they've gathered by the big haystack. There's another big storm coming and I thought we ought to start feeding. According to the weatherman, there's supposed to be a big storm coming about every three days until the end of the month. That's the forecast. I've already got three men down at the cabin by the haystack to start feeding. I thought I'd move you down there where you'd be closer to the cattle when the calving gets going full swing."

"It won't take me long to gather up my stuff an' move," I said. "All I've got is extra clothes and my bedroll."

"We'll need to take the canned goods and groceries. The men already have plenty of food there, but we'll take what's here anyway. I'll take you and your stuff in the truck, then come back and get your horse."

"You'll need to come back an' get the cow an' calf I've got in the shed," I said.

We gathered up the groceries, my extra clothes and bedroll, loaded them in the truck and started out. I didn't much like the idea of changing camp in the middle of winter, but apparently it was Phil's idea and he thought it needed to be done.

"You needed the plow to get out here?" I asked.

"Yes. I had to buck some pretty deep snowdrifts. I'll plow a little more on the way back."

As we drove, Phil widened the plowed road with the plow.

"You'll have a four lane highway out here by the time you're done," I remarked.

"That's all right," replied Phil. "I don't want to get stuck. I almost did in a couple of places coming out."

I saw where Phil had plowed the snow off the road and piled it to the side. In a couple of places, I saw where he'd got off the road completely. Occasionally, he'd drop the blade and plow more.

"I think you're just a frustrated heavy equipment operator," I said, as Phil improved the plowing job he'd already done. Phil just grinned.

After about three hours of driving and plowing, we arrived at the cabin, but nobody was around. There was a set of corrals and an old shed there.

"This was an old homestead. I suppose the men are out feeding," said Phil. There was a truck parked by the cabin.

"What are they feedin' with?" I asked.

"There's a tractor and a flatbed trailer."

We unloaded the groceries and my stuff and put them in the cabin. The cabin was still warm so the men hadn't been gone long. There was an extra bunk in the cabin.

"That'll be yours," said Phil.

We put my bedroll and extra clothes on the empty bunk and went back to the truck.

"Now we'll go back and get your horse," said Phil.

3

We went to the truck and started back to my original camp. We made better time going back, as Phil didn't spend much time improving the snowplowing job he'd already done.

When we got back to my camp, I saddled my horse and we loaded him in the truck. I threw the cow enough hay to keep her overnight. Heading back to the old homestead, Phil said, "I'll come back for the cow and calf tomorrow."

After getting to the old homestead, I unloaded the horse, unsaddled him and put him in the corral. I threw him some hay, it was too late in the day to go out and check cattle. Phil went to the cabin.

The three men that had been feeding cattle came out of the cabin and were standing on the porch talking with Phil when I headed to the cabin. There was some loud language and animated conversation on the porch between the three men. Phil appeared to be listening, but not joining in the talk.

I listened as I approached. One of the men was saying, "An' he don't do his share of the work! I load twice as much hay as he does! He's a lazy, no good!"

"You watch your language, Jack! You know that with this bum leg, I don't get around good! I do as much as I'm capable of."

"Bum leg! Bull!" retorted Jack. "I've seen you walk when you think no one's watchin' an' you get along as good as anybody! You're fakin'. An' how come it takes you as long to do dishes as it takes Frank an' me to load hay in the mornin'? Just fakin' is all you're doin'!"

"I notice that you're no speed ball when you do dishes!"

"But I do 'em fast enough to come out an' help load hay!" replied Jack. "An' they're clean when I get done with 'em!"

Phil interrupted. "What's the situation Frank?"

"Well," replied Frank, "they're both right! Rocky says he has to drive the tractor 'cause of his bum leg and Jack and I have been forking off the hay. It's only been two days, and they've been constantly arguing all the time. This would be a lot better job if they were split up. And Rocky hasn't loaded much hay."

"You know that ain't right!" replied Rocky.

"That's right," chimed in Jack.

The two antagonists seemed to partner up when Frank had words against them both.

"That's the way I see it!" answered Frank.

"Well," said Phil, "I guess I ought to take one of you with me back to the ranch. Who wants to go?"

"I do," said Jack.

"Me too!" said Rocky.

"Fine," said Phil. "I'll take both of you back and you can hit the road when we get to the ranch. Get your stuff and put it in the truck. I'll have your paychecks ready."

Jack and Rocky went into the cabin and started to gather up their belongings.

Phil turned to me and said, "Do you mind helping Frank for a few days until I can hire someone to replace these two? You can check the cows when you're helping Frank feed."

"I suppose not," I said. "Looks like to me it has to be done."

"Good," replied Phil. "I'll get someone out here as soon as I can hire them."

Phil introduced me to Frank. As the introductions progressed and Frank and I were getting acquainted, Rocky came out of the cabin carrying his bedroll. As he walked by Frank, he bumped into him, making him step back. He continued on his way, not bothering to apologize to Frank.

I could see Frank get a little upset and said, "He's not very courteous, is he."

"No," answered Frank. "Not at all. It'll be good to have him and his partner gone."

"They're partners?" I asked.

"Yep. They came in together and got hired together. Strange partners, they're always arguing about something, no matter how small it is."

"Some people are like that," I said. "It seems like they have to be complaining about something all the time just to justify their existence."

Jack put his belongings in the back of the truck. He and Rocky were arguing about who was going to sit by the door on the way back to the ranch.

Phil said to me, as he headed to the truck, "I'll bring you another horse when I come back." Then he said, "You boys get in. When I get in, I'm going, with or without you! And I don't want to hear any arguing on the way home! In fact, I don't want to hear anything from either one of you! If I hear as much as a squeak from either one, I'll let you out and you can walk the rest of the way!"

I could see that Phil wasn't too happy with either one of them. Phil got in the truck and Rocky pushed Jack in the truck. Rocky was closing the door as Phil drove off. Phil meant business!

Frank went inside the cabin. "I'll start supper," he said.

I followed Frank into the cabin and checked my gear, thinking Jack or Rocky might have taken some of it. Everything was there, as near as I could tell.

"Seein' as you're fixin' supper," I said, "I'll do the dishes when we're done."

"I appreciate that. That's more than either one of them other two guys volunteered to do. They were both lazy and their arguments were mostly about who was the worst. Actually, they were about the same. They're the kind that makes a pretty fair living panhandling out on some corner."

I didn't say anything and patiently waited for supper to be done. Frank fixed up a pretty good meal, leastways it was better than my own cooking. I was getting pretty tired of it.

I did the dishes and Frank and I visited a little

before we turned in. I thought he was all right and would be good to work with.

The next morning, Frank was up before I was and had the fire going.

"It's real nice to get up when it's startin' to warm up," I said. "Where I was camped, I'd have to get up in the middle of the night an' get the fire goin' again. Then, I'd have to restart it in the mornin'. This is almost like havin' a personal valet," I added jokingly.

Frank laughed. "Don't be thinking that!" he said. "Anytime you get cold during the night, feel free to get up and add to the fire. I got up around two this morning and did it."

"You want me to fix breakfast?" I asked.

"Nope," replied Frank. "You can cook your own eggs the way you like them. I've started the bacon. I've got some sourdough and I'd prefer nobody messed with it. I'll fix up some pancakes. You just relax and get ready to work. The coffee's about ready."

"I can do that," I said, as I poured myself a cup.

When we finished breakfast, I did the dishes. Then we bundled up and went outside to load the trailer and feed. It was cold and the frost in the air shined and sparkled in the sunlight.

We could see our breath as we walked to the tractor.

Frank climbed onto the seat and tried to start the tractor. Nothing happened. He let out a string of cuss words that more than adequately described Jack's ancestry and him.

"That good for nothing Jack left the key on the accessory," said Frank. "The battery's dead. There's a set of jumper cables in the truck. Bring it over and we'll get this thing going."

I went to the pickup, hoping the battery in the truck wasn't dead. It wasn't. I drove the pickup over to the tractor and we got it started. Frank drove the tractor to the stack yard and we loaded hay.

"We'll put about thirty bales on each layer," said Frank. "The first layer is the only one we'll have to throw bales up to. After it's loaded, we'll move the tractor up and we can throw the bales down onto it. You stack, I'll throw the hay. I'll leave the tractor running to charge up the battery." Frank had to brush snow off each bale before he loaded it so he could find the strings.

We loaded hay. There was a pitchfork on the trailer and I had to move it out of the way each time we started a new layer. Frank moved the tractor up and I stayed on the trailer. The way it was working out, I could see that I was going to pitch the hay to the cattle.

When we had five tiers of hay loaded, about a hundred and fifty bales, Frank said, "That's enough. We'll feed this then come back for a second load. Before I left the ranch, I welded a knife from the mowing machine on the fork. Use it to cut the strings. I'll get the gate, you just stay up there and enjoy the hayride."

I laughed. "Some hayride!" I said. "It's colder than a mother-in-law's kiss!"

Frank laughed and we started out.

We started feeding cattle. Each time I finished feeding a layer of hay, I'd have Frank stop and I'd cut and pull the hay strings. It wasn't long before we had the first load of hay fed and were headed back to the stack yard. Frank put the trailer in place.

"You throw the hay and I'll stack. Then it'll be your turn to drive."

"Why don't you drive again?" I asked. "You know the lay of the ground and where to go. I don't, an' I don't want to get us stuck."

"Suit yourself," said Frank. "We've fed this first load a lot faster than when there were three of us feeding!"

"That's probably because I ain't got anybody

to argue with, except myself," I said. "An' I hate to do that because I never can tell who won!"

Frank laughed and slapped me on the back. "You'll do!" he said.

We loaded the trailer again with about a hundred and fifty bales of hay. When we were done loading, Frank asked, "You want to stop for dinner?"

"No," I said. "Why don't we feed this, then break for dinner? After we eat, we can come out and load up again."

"This is all we have to feed. That'll be three hundred bales and there's just under six hundred cows. I figure about a half a bale per cow."

"Let's feed this, then we can load up for tomorrow after we eat," I said.

"I like your thinking," said Frank. "The other two guys were always looking to put off the work until later."

We fed the second load then went to the cabin for dinner.

"Seeing as you did all the forking off, I'll fix dinner," said Frank, as he started a fire in the stove.

"I'll go to the barn an' throw my horse some hay while you're doin' that," I said. "I threw him plenty yesterday."

The horse hadn't cleaned up the hay I fed him the day before, so I gave him a little less this time. I spent some extra time with the horse, I didn't want to get in Frank's way while he was fixing dinner.

When I returned to the cabin, dinner was about ready. We ate in silence and when we were through Frank said, "I think we ought to let this settle for a time. Then we can go out and load up for tomorrow."

"Suits me," I said. "I'll just relax on my bunk. I generally don't sleep during the day, but if I fall asleep, don't be afraid to wake me up!"

I layed down on the bunk and before I knew it, Frank was calling me, "Wake up! Wake up! It's time to load up!"

I'd fallen asleep, even though I'd slept well the night before. I was surprised that I woke up wanting more sleep.

"You were really sawing some logs," said Frank. "You slept for about an hour."

"Did you get any sleep?" I asked.

"Yep. Seems like coming in from the cold and getting real warm tends to put a feller to sleep real fast."

"Let's go get loaded," I said, as I pulled on my over boots.

"We ain't going to town," said Frank, laughing at his own joke.

I grinned. I had no intention of going to town nor did I even want to. I was content where I was even though it was cold.

We loaded the hay for the first feeding in the morning. Frank threw the hay to me on the trailer and I stacked it. As we walked back to the cabin, Frank remarked, "You know, those two guys, Rocky and Jack, were so lazy, that we actually ended up spending more time out in the cold. Then they continually complained about how cold it was. I don't think they worked hard enough to even warm up!"

"The hardest part of any job, it seems to me, is the gettin' started. I'd just as soon get started then get done, particularly the harder, more distasteful jobs."

"Are you saying you want me to throw hay faster?" asked Frank, grinning.

"Nope. I don't want to work so fast that I'd build up a sweat. Just fast enough to keep warm!"

Two days later, Phil showed up with two more hands. He also had another horse in the back of the truck.

"These two hands will help Frank feed and you can go back to checking cattle horseback," said Phil, as he unloaded the horse. "The horse is Diamond. He's as honest as the day is long. He'll do you a good job.

"The two new men are Mike and Angelo," continued Phil, as he handed me the horse.

Frank and I shook hands with the two new men. Frank apparently knew Angelo. As he shook his hand, he said, "It's good to see you again. I guess you didn't make it back home this winter."

"No, I didn't," replied Angelo. In broken English, he continued, "I started but ran out of money. This job came up and I am here."

I put the horse in the corral, threw both horses enough hay to keep them fed overnight and went back to the cabin. The four men were inside talking as I entered.

Phil saw me and said, "You've got about another week until the cows start calving steady. There's supposed to be a storm coming day after tomorrow, so be ready."

I grunted a "Yep," and poured myself a cup of coffee. "For some reason or other, them calves like to be born during bad weather."

Phil said, "I'll be bringing up more groceries in a few days," and left.

The next day, I was anxious to try out the new

horse, so I got up early, started the fire, put the coffee on, and was about to head to the barn. Frank was just getting up as I was walking out the door.

"Going to get an early start," said Frank.

"Yep. Coffee's started."

4

I caught Diamond, hobbled and saddled him as he ate his grain. I grained the other horse. Diamond acted decent and didn't even hump up as I tightened the cinch. I took off the nosebags and took the hobbles off Diamond, threw the horses some hay, then went to the cabin to eat breakfast.

"Cold out there this morning?" asked Mike as I entered the cabin. The three men were seated at the table eating.

"Yep," I answered. "But it don't feel as cold as it was yesterday. Maybe it's warmin' up ahead of this new storm comin' in."

"Don't count on it," said Frank. "Breakfast is on the stove. You'll have to cook your own eggs."

I got breakfast and as I ate, I said, "I'll be gettin' up early to check the cattle. I'll start the coffee but I won't eat until after I've been through the cattle, so leave the coffee on when you leave."

"You be eating a brunch, then?" asked Frank.

"What's a brunch?" I asked.

"Brunch is a meal between breakfast and lunch," replied Frank. "It's real popular among businessmen in the city."

"Where I come from the noon meal is dinner, not lunch. I'm not a businessman from the city, so I guess I'll be eatin' brinner!"

Frank laughed. "Whatever you call it, the coffee will be on when you come back. We've got some time before we start feeding. I guess we'll wait until it warms up some more before we start."

I went outside, untracked Diamond, cheeked him, and stepped on him, expecting the worst. He was a new horse to me and I never knew what to expect from a new horse. But he acted decent and we went out and checked cows.

Other than being very cold there wasn't anything new. The sun was up, but it wasn't warming up very fast. The cow and calf I'd brought to the shed at the other camp were doing well.

I said out loud to the calf, "It won't be long before you start gettin' some playmates." I rode for about two hours without seeing any cows that were about to calve or needing assistance and headed back to the cabin. I saw Frank, Angelo, and Mike shoveling off hay to the cattle as I rode to the cabin. Frank was driving the tractor and Angelo and Mike were shoveling off the hay, each one on one side of the trailer. *They'll be done in half the time it took Frank an' me to feed,* I thought.

I got to the barn and turned Diamond loose in the corral. I left him saddled, figuring on riding him later that day and went to the cabin to eat.

The fire had gone out in the stove and the coffee was only lukewarm. I started the fire and went to fixing a meal. I didn't know whether to have breakfast or dinner. There was some cold bacon left from the other men's breakfast, so I decided to have breakfast.

After I ate, I did the dishes. The other men had done their dishes, so I didn't have much to do. I heard the tractor coming into the yard, and I started another pot of coffee. The men came in and we visited for a while.

"It don't take as much time to feed with these two guys as it did you and me," said Frank.

"Of course not," I replied. "You have 'em shovelin' hay off both sides of the trailer!"

"Pretty soon we'll move the feed ground out across the creek and open up some new ground," said Frank. "It'll take a little longer to travel out there."

"How come we cross the creek?" asked Angelo.

"We're scattering the manure from the cows naturally," said Frank.

"So," I said, "You're not cattle feeders, you're manure spreaders!"

Frank laughed. "I guess you're right. We'll warm up a little then go load the hay for feeding this afternoon. You going to eat with us?"

"No," I replied. "I just finished eatin' my brinner an' ain't got room. But I should be in early enough to eat supper with you."

Frank, Angelo and Mike went out to load hay and I relaxed in the cabin. It was warm and I fell asleep for a spell. When I awoke, Mike was fixing the noon meal and Frank and Angelo were talking.

"I was wondering when you were going to wake up," said Frank.

"I guess I dozed off a little," I said. "That's kinda unusual for me. I generally can't sleep during the middle of the day."

"Your horse was laying down when we came in," said Frank. "I got him up, but you've got some cleaning to do on your saddle."

"Thanks," I said. "I appreciate it. I guess I'll have to unsaddle him in the future."

After cleaning off my saddle, I rode through

44

the cattle later in the day and didn't find any cows that needed help calving. In the evening, when I was done for the day, I brought my saddle blankets and pad into the cabin. I didn't want the frozen pad and blankets to be causing a saddle sore on either one of my horses.

The next few days were pretty much the same, although there were a few calves starting to show up.

One day, I was completing my morning rounds when I heard yelling coming from the creek. I figured the yelling was for me as there wasn't anyone else around, so I rode over to see what the commotion was about.

Mike was on the tractor in the middle of the creek. Frank and Angelo were on the trailer. They were stuck. They had broken through the ice and the tractor wheels were just spinning on the frozen ground. A lot of cattle were behind the trailer waiting to be fed.

"We just need a little help," said Mike. "Can you and your horse give us a little pull to help regain our traction so we can get going again?"

"I suppose," I said. "But I don't want to step off into that cold water."

I rode over to the tractor and handed my lariat rope to Mike.

"Put this on the front some place an' I'll see if we can't make it move. It'll be tough, you've got a full load of hay on the trailer."

Mike looked disdainfully at the creek as he took my rope. "That water's going to be cold," he said.

"Maybe you can crawl out on the hood an' hook onto the front axle without gettin' wet," I said.

I grinned as I watched Mike crawling along the hood. If he fell, he'd get soaking wet in the creek.

Mike took the rope, uncoiled it, took the end out of the hondo and dropped the hondo down alongside the axle.

"I can't reach it to loop it around the axle," he said.

I rode my horse over to the front of the tractor, leaned out of the saddle, and grabbed the hondo. I put the end of the rope around the front axle, through the hondo, then rode out of the creek and dallied up.

"Give her some gas," I hollered.

Mike gave the tractor some gas and we took the slack out of the rope. The tractor moved slightly forward then rolled back.

"We'll get her rocking and get out of here," yelled Mike.

After a few attempts, we got the tractor unstuck. The tractor came out of the creek so fast, I had to spur my horse out of the way. Mike kept going until the trailer got out of the creek.

On solid ground, Mike got off the tractor, released my rope from the axle and handed me the end.

"I'd find another place to cross goin' back," I said. "With all the cows followin' you, it'll be tougher to cross here goin' back."

"Sure," said Mike, as he climbed back on the tractor.

I coiled my rope and rode back to the barn. At the barn, I unsaddled the horse, threw him some hay and went to the cabin. I started fixing my "brinner."

I was getting used to the routine; up early in the morning, check the cattle, go back to the cabin, eat a late breakfast, rest a little then go out early in the afternoon to check the cattle again. I didn't have far to ride, the cattle were generally gathered on the feed grounds. If I did see a cow off and away from the herd, I would ride over and see if she was about to calve or had calved.

If she was about to calve, I was ready to help her if she needed help.

It continued to stay cold and I didn't really look forward to taking off my coat, rolling up my sleeves to try to turn a calf around if it was hung up in the birth canal. Generally, I just had to pull a calf's front feet until its head came out and I didn't have to take off my coat to do that.

One day, Phil showed up with more groceries. The other men were out feeding, and I was in the cabin fixing my late breakfast.

"Having brunch, huh?" asked Phil as he entered the cabin.

"Nope," I said. "This is brinner."

"Brinner? What's that?"

"It's the meal between breakfast and dinner," I replied.

Phil laughed. "That's a new one on me! Soon as you get done with your brinner, ah, that is, ah, your meal, come out and help me bring in your groceries."

"Sure," I said. "Grab yourself a cup of coffee while you're waitin'. You want somethin' to eat?"

"No, coffee will do." Phil poured himself a cup of coffee and sat down at the table. When my eggs were done, I joined him and we talked as I ate.

"I figure we're about a quarter done calvin'," I said. "I've had to help a few cows."

"That's about where we should be," said Phil. "I guess we're right on schedule. How many have you lost?"

"There's three that I know of," I said. "Two were either born dead or froze an' one was comin' out backward an' I couldn't get him out fast enough. That's all that I know of."

"That's not bad," said Phil. "I really expected more. How's your horses holding up?"

"They're doin' fine," I replied. "I'm usin' one in the mornin' an' the other one durin' the afternoon. By the way, what do you call them?"

"Diamond is the last one I brought you," answered Phil.

"I know that," I interrupted. "You never told me the name of the other one."

"The other one is Buster."

"Buster, huh?"

"Yes," replied Phil. "I named him that after he fell on me and broke my leg three years ago while I was breaking him."

I immediately thought of that morning when he bucked and fell with me at the other camp.

"I couldn't finish breaking him until my leg

healed. Even then, my wife had some misgivings about me finishing the job. But I did."

I finished eating and Phil and I brought the groceries inside the cabin. When we were done, Phil said, "Let's go drive through the cattle. I'd like to see how they're doing. It's been an unusually cold winter."

"It would be nice to look at them from a warm truck," I said. "It's been plenty cold out here."

We drove out to the cattle. "Why don't you check cattle from the pickup?" asked Phil.

"It would certainly be warmer," I replied, "but I wouldn't be able to assist any cows needin' help."

"I see," said Phil.

Phil was satisfied when he looked at the cattle and we followed Frank, Angelo, and Mike back to the cabin.

There was considerable cussing from Mike when we entered the cabin. In between cuss words I managed to gather that Mike was cussing the weather. It had become colder and I figured that was because the nights were clear. There were no clouds to trap the warm air from the day and it escaped into the atmosphere.

"The cold is because of a temperature inversion," Phil was saying.

"What's that?" asked Mike.

"That's when the cold air becomes trapped next to the earth by the warm air above it," replied Phil. "It'll stay cold until the warm air moves on allowing the cold air to move on."

"But ten below zero when the sun is shining is a little extreme," said Mike, with some cuss words conveniently placed in his statement for effect. "I much prefer warmer weather."

"Don't worry," said Frank, "where you're headed, it'll be plenty warm."

Phil, Angelo and I laughed.

Gradually, the days got warmer. The ground was still frozen and what snow that had melted formed little water pools in the low spots on the ground. These little pools would freeze at night and melt during the heat of the day. Around ten or eleven o'clock in the morning when the ice melted, the feed grounds became a quagmire.

Frank cussed the cold weather. The quagmire on the ground made it necessary to drive the tractor at a faster speed when feeding. The tractor tires would throw mud, water, and manure back on the hay wagon and quite often, on the feeders. Even when a new area was opened up to feed, it didn't take long for the new ground to become as bad as the old ground. The ground was slick and the tractor would slide around, jerking the trailer in unexpected directions. More than once, one of the men throwing off hay was thrown off the trailer due to the trailer being jerked around. Quite often, the men would come in from feeding covered with mud and manure.

Often, when I came into the cabin in the evening, I would find all three men seated at the table in their long johns, playing cards. Their wet clothes were scattered around, draped over various articles of furniture in an effort to dry them out.

Slowly, but surely, the days started warming up. The nights were cold, still below freezing, and the snow that had melted the day before froze during the night. The following day, everything that had frozen thawed out, making the ground slick all over. I began to wonder if I would ever see dry, unfrozen ground again.

The calving was going nicely. New calves were appearing every morning. I did lose a few calves. Some of the calves had chosen to be born backward and if I couldn't get them out fast enough, they would drown in their own amniotic fluid. But, I did manage to save a few calves. I was fortunate that none of the cows rejected their calves. I didn't have a corral where I could keep them and force feed the calves until the cows accepted them.

I wasn't happy that I had lost a few calves and I was lamenting this when Phil showed up with more groceries. As I helped him take the groceries into the cabin, he tried to console me by saying, "Don't feel too bad. We've never had a hundred percent calving percentage."

"But I feel like I let you down losin' a few calves," I said. "If I'd have gotten to some of them cows a little quicker, I could have saved a few more calves."

"You did the best you could, didn't you?" asked Phil.

"Certainly," I replied, "but …"

Phil cut me off. "Then don't feel bad. If you did your best, that's all I can expect."

Phil appeared satisfied. He was the boss, the owner, and apparently he was happy with my performance. And I *had* done my best. My two horses were showing signs of being overworked. A few weeks rest would do them both some good.

"This is the toughest winter we've ever had," said Phil. "I'm sure glad we had a good deal of hay stored. It would have been rough if we'd have had to buy hay."

5

Each passing day seemed to bring more warmth, although the nights were still cold. The days had warmed up enough that a feller thought about leaving his heavy winter coat at home. But the mornings were still cold and when the sun started dipping in the west in the late afternoon, a feller was glad he'd brought the coat along.

I learned a lesson one morning when it was starting to warm up. I had my heavy coat on and it became uncomfortably warm. I decided to take off my coat and started to, but that action spooked Buster and he started bucking. He did a better job of bucking than he'd done back at my camp.

With my coat half on and half off, I couldn't do a very good job of riding the horse, and I couldn't do a very good job of holding on. Buster bucked me off! I landed, face down, in the muddy, wet feed grounds. As soon as Buster realized he'd unloaded me, he headed for home.

Without thinking, I rolled over and sat up. I checked for broken bones and was relieved to not find any, although I was sore. In rolling over, I completed the job of thoroughly getting myself soaked, on both sides and front and back. *This is a fine mess,* I thought. I got up and started walking back to the cabin. There was a little wind blowing and I thought it might be helpful in drying me off. It wasn't much help in drying me off, but it did have a chilling effect.

I'd walked for about fifteen minutes and saw Frank, Angelo, and Mike feeding the last load of hay for the day. I hollered at them and got them to stop and wait for me. I still had about a mile's walk back to the cabin and wasn't looking forward to it.

All three of the guys had big grins on their faces when I got to the tractor and trailer.

"You want to join our long john poker club?" asked Angelo in his heavily accented English.

"Very funny," I said disgustedly, as I climbed on the trailer.

"We saw your horse go by without you," said Frank, from the seat of the tractor. "We were going to finish feeding this, then come looking for you. Looks like you found us. What happened?"

"I lost my horse."

"We can see that," said Frank.

"I was takin' off my coat an' my horse come uncorked. He dumped me."

"Well, your horse had sense enough to head for home," said Mike.

"Yeah," I said. "But he should have waited for me!"

I rode the trailer back to the bunkhouse. I wished Frank would have driven faster; my wet clothes weren't keeping me very warm. When we got to the barn, I saw Buster standing at the gate to the corral, waiting for me.

As I walked over to him to unsaddle him, I asked him, "You were in such a rush to get home, why didn't you unsaddle yourself?"

I unsaddled Buster, turned him loose in the corral, threw him some hay and went to the bunkhouse. I shed my wet clothes, laid out some clean, dry clothes on my bunk, grabbed a towel and headed for the shower.

I relished in the shower as the warm water warmed me up. I didn't remember being so cold before and was reluctant to get out. However, all good things must end, and I got out. I think I'll always remember how cold I was and how that hot shower warmed me up.

By the time I got dressed, Angelo had supper ready. After a hot shower, a hot meal hit the spot. I didn't worry about overheating!

Spring was slow in coming, but it was gradually warming up. It wasn't long before the temperature during the nights wasn't dipping below zero. The days were actually nice and I started wearing a lighter jacket rather than my heavy winter coat.

One day, Phil, the ranch owner, came up to me and asked, "We about done calving yet?"

"Yep," I answered.

"What are your plans when we're done here?"

"I really hadn't made any plans," I replied. "I figured I'd stick around at least till you're done brandin'."

"We can sure use you branding. We'll have a lot of calves to brand. Then there won't be much to do other than help in the hay. You want to do that?"

"I ain't really too much interested in drivin' a tractor around all day," I answered. I didn't want to tell Phil that I was too much a cowboy or buckaroo to be put on a tractor. I was pretty prideful and proud to be what I was.

"Maybe we could find a few colts for you to break," replied Phil.

"I could hang around for that," I said. "How many you got?"

"There's four three-year-olds. They've been halter broke and broke to lead. They're all big, strong young horses. They'll need plenty of riding. I'd like to have them broke good enough that Mike and Frank could ride them."

"Given enough time, I could have 'em so as your mother could ride 'em," I said. "Don't you want Angelo to ride?"

"You'll have all summer if you want," said Phil. "Angelo is going back to Mexico. His work permit expires soon."

"Oh. Where are the horses? I haven't seen any other horses around here but Buster an' Diamond."

"They're at the home ranch," replied Phil. "You'll see them when we bring the cattle in to brand. I'll bring a couple of gentle horses out for Mike and Frank to ride to help bring the cattle in. They haven't rode much. Angelo will bring the tractor and trailer. I'll come back later with someone and bring back the pickup."

"When do you want to start?" I asked.

"We're done calving for the most part. I'll

bring out horses next week and you can start the cattle home. It'll take four days to reach the corrals, but there's some holding pastures along the way where you can keep the cattle at night. Angelo will lead, the cattle should follow the feed trailer and make it pretty easy. You'll have to camp out under the stars each night. You can put your bedroll on the trailer."

"Frank an' Mike don't have bedrolls?" I asked.

"Their bedrolls will be on the trailer also, along with the groceries."

About a week later, Phil showed up with two horses and two old saddles in the back of the truck. The horses were old and just by looking at them I knew Phil didn't figure Frank or Mike to be much of a horseman.

I met Phil as he got out of the truck. "Are those two old timers capable of makin' the trip?"

"I hope so," replied Phil. "They're two old pensioners just living out their days here. I don't think the exercise will hurt them; might do them some good. You'll be moving pretty slow with all the calves."

"There hasn't been any new calves born since you were here last week," I said.

"Good! It's time to go. You can start in the

morning. It should take you about four days to get to the home ranch, just taking your time. I'll have the boys load up the trailer with hay."

The next morning, I rolled up my bedroll with my extra clothes inside it and placed it by the door. "Don't forget this," I said as I went out to saddle my horse.

Angelo nodded and said, "Si amigo."

I had Diamond saddled by the time Frank and Mike showed up. I helped them saddle their horses, then caught Buster and gave him to Frank to lead during the day. Then we started out to gather cattle.

I made the big circle and pushed cattle toward Frank and Mike. After half a day, we had the herd started toward the home ranch. I got Buster from Frank and took him to Angelo and the tractor and trailer. I changed horses, tied Diamond to the back of the trailer, told Angelo to take it easy and went back to the herd. Cows were starting to follow the tractor and trailer.

I rode back to Mike and Frank and said, "We'll take 'em plenty slow. We don't want all the calves in the rear. The cows will want to spread out an' I'll keep 'em lined out proper. Don't let anything behind you!"

Watching Mike and Frank, I could tell they hadn't worked with cattle much, but they were bringing up the rear and doing a fair job. They did a lot of back-tracking, but as near as I could tell, they hadn't left anything behind. Along toward evening, we came to the first holding pasture. We turned the cattle in there and went about setting up an overnight camp.

Angelo started a fire, Mike and Frank unsaddled their horses, tied them to the wagon and spread out their bedrolls on the ground. I went out and rustled up some firewood. I found a good-sized fallen aspen tree and I dragged it back to where we were setting up camp.

Angelo had gone to the creek and got some water. Mike and Frank were stretched out on their bedrolls.

"Don't you think you fellers ought to water your horses?" I asked. "They ain't had a drink all day."

Looking somewhat guilty, Mike and Frank got up, untied their horses and started leading them over to the creek. I rode over to the trailer, untied Diamond and led him to water. I let both horses get their fill. Frank and Mike showed up leading their horses.

"Make sure they get plenty," I said. "An'

tomorrow, give 'em a chance to drink every time we cross the creek."

The next day, we got an early start. As soon as we ate breakfast, Angelo started packing up the cooking supplies. I threw my bedroll on the trailer, saddled Buster and started out to gather cattle. As I left, I heard Angelo tell Mike and Frank, in his broken English, "If you amigos want your bedrolls, you better put them on the trailer. I am not your mother."

I rode over to where Frank was rolling up his bedroll and said, "You and Mike wait at the gate. I'll gather the cattle an' push 'em toward it. You guys turn 'em toward the ranch. Would you mind leading Diamond for me? I think Angelo might drive too fast for the horse to keep up."

"Sure," replied Frank.

The holding pasture wasn't big and it didn't take long to get the cattle gathered and headed toward the ranch. I started the cattle toward the gate. Frank and Mike were in place. The cattle headed toward the home ranch and from the way some of the cattle started running, they knew where they were going.

I got to the gate, got off Buster and closed it. Mike and Frank were waiting. "We'll do just like yesterday. You guys follow an' I'll keep 'em pointed the right direction. Keep 'em movin' real easy, I think some of the calves got a little tired yesterday. If you have any problems, come an' get me."

The men nodded and I left to keep any possible bunch quitters from leaving and slow the leaders down a little. I didn't have too tough a job, we had a fence on the east side all the way to the ranch.

Along toward noon, Angelo had stopped, made a fire, and started fixing a noon meal. He'd passed the herd after he broke camp. I stopped the leaders and held them after they passed the tractor. I figured we'd stop the whole herd past the tractor and trailer, then we could see any calves or cows trying to go back while we ate.

I went back to help Frank and Mike push the last of the cattle past the truck. We watched them for a while. A lot of the calves laid down to rest while the cows grazed. It seemed like the cattle were contented, there wasn't much milling around and a lot of the cows had located their calves or knew where they were. We went back to the truck to eat the noon meal.

Angelo had a good meal fixed and as we ate, he said, "The next holding pasture is about four hours away. I'll open the gate and start supper. I'll be ready for you when you get there."

"That can't be too soon," said Mike. "I'm still stiff and sore from yesterday!"

While we ate, we watched the cattle. There weren't any that tried to go back. After eating, Angelo loaded his supplies on the trailer and started out. I switched horses, had Frank lead Buster, and started out toward the leaders.

Some of the leaders had drifted toward the ranch and I slowed them down so we could keep somewhat of a semblance of a herd.

Around midday, Frank came trotting up toward me. He looked like he was having a hard time staying in the saddle as he got closer to me.

"What's up?" I asked

"There's a cow down. She looks like she's trying to calve and having a tough time. You better come back."

"Okay," I answered. "Where's Buster?"

"Mike's leading him."

"Okay, I'll hurry back," I said. "You can take your time. You looked like you weren't enjoyin' the ride up here too much."

As I rode back to where Mike was waiting, I thought to myself, *Them guys ain't much good as cowboys. Cattle feeders! That's what they are.*

I got to Mike. He was sitting on his horse, holding Buster, and he had a big grin on his face.

"It's all done," he said. "And I got to watch it!"

I looked over at the cow lying on the ground, resting. Behind her was a newborn calf, breathing heavily with his head slowly bobbing up and down. The cow hadn't gotten up yet to clean off the calf.

I surveyed the situation and decided there wasn't anything I could do.

I turned to Mike and said, "Well, it looks like you've become a father! Congratulations!"

"That's the first one I ever seen born. That's something!" Mike was really impressed with the event.

"That's something to see your first born being born. You should feel proud! He looks just like you, but where'd the red hair come from?"

"Bull," retorted Mike.

"We'll leave both him an' his mom here for a few days, until he's able to travel. I'll come back an' get 'em later. Can you leave your newborn alone with his ma for a few days?"

"You go to blazes!"

Mike was getting a little upset, although I was only teasing him. I decided I'd better stop. I didn't realize he was so sensitive.

"We better leave 'em alone to get acquainted," I said. "If you can drag yourself away, just keep following the herd. I'll go up an' keep the leaders lined out an' send Frank back."

I left Mike and started back toward the leaders. When I got to Frank, I found the leaders scattered. It was apparent that Frank didn't know what to do. I sent him back to Mike and slowly pushed the leaders back in the direction they were supposed to go.

We made slow progress during the afternoon but finally reached the holding pasture. Angelo had parked the truck in such a manner that helped turn the cattle into the pasture. He'd started fixing supper.

I hadn't got a count on the cattle, as too many cattle had entered the pasture before I got there. I resolved to get a count before we got to the ranch.

Frank and Mike arrived, pushing the stragglers. I closed the gate after we watered our horses. I rode back and got Diamond and led him to water. After he got a good drink, I rode back to where Angelo had fixed supper, hobbled both horses and turned them loose to graze. Then I went to feed myself.

6

Before we turned in that night, Phil showed up. He'd brought some more supplies. We sat around visiting for a while and finally Phil said, "You should be at the home ranch in two more days. We'll turn the cattle out on the hay fields and go to branding the next day."

"Two more days!" exclaimed Mike. "I don't know if I can last that long!"

"You'll make it," I reassured him. "After all, you've got a family to look out for!" I couldn't help but tease Mike, but he didn't take it well.

"What's this about a family?" asked Phil.

I explained that a calf had been born and we had to leave him and his mother behind. "When we get to the home ranch, I'll come back an' get 'em."

"That won't be necessary," said Phil. "They'll find their way home in time. We've got the neighbors coming to help brand the next three days. It'll take us that long. Try to get a count on the cows as they go into the hay fields."

"Whatever you say."

The next day went pretty much like the previous days. I got a fairly accurate count on the cows that night as they went into another holding pasture. We watered the horses and tied them to the truck. We were close enough to the home ranch that I thought they might try to go home early. We had plenty of hay on the wagon.

The next day would be our last day trailing cattle. It hadn't been too difficult; we had a fence on one side all the way. I surveyed the crew. Angelo was in good shape. He'd driven the truck and set up camp and cooked each day.

Frank and Mike were a different story. They weren't used to riding horseback. Frank was holding up pretty well, even though he was a little saddle sore. Mike was in pretty rough shape. He was really saddle sore and quite often, as I looked back to see how the herd was coming, I would see him walking on foot, leading his horse. He wasn't used to riding and apparently hadn't done any in the past. I kinda felt sorry for him. But we had managed. The cattle were in good shape, although some of the younger calves were becoming a little tired, even though Frank and Mike hadn't pushed the stragglers hard.

The next day, I told Frank and Mike to take it easy with the herd. It would be our last day and we needed to get all the cattle in the holding pasture. I'd slow the leaders down and get another count on them as they went into the pasture. I wanted to verify my count from the day before. I told Angelo to keep the gate closed until I got there so I could count all the cattle.

When I got to the gate to the holding pasture, Angelo hadn't opened it and the cattle were milling around outside the pasture. Phil was there helping Angelo hold the cattle. He wasn't horseback, he was on a four-wheeler.

As I rode up to the gate, I noticed a lot of pickups, trailers and campers inside the holding pasture. There were some temporary pens set up and unsaddled horses inside them. The place really looked like a county fair parking lot. The only things missing were a Ferris wheel, merry-go-round, and a Midway, with barkers hollering out, "Come try your skill and win a prize!" I was surprised at the conglomeration. People were walking around and there were a lot of kids running around. There were a number of campfires sending up small spirals of smoke scattered around the area. Other than a baseball game being played on the far side of the camp, the area did look somewhat like a fairgrounds.

I rode up to the gate, opened it and started counting the cattle through. Phil started counting on the other side. When Frank and Mike finally pushed the last of the cattle through the gate, Mike got off his horse and closed the gate.

"Finally!" he said. "That's a relief!" He could hardly walk, he was so stiff from riding the last four days. "I think I'm crippled for life! It won't bother me if I never get on a horse again!"

Phil was laughing at Mike as he walked toward me and he asked me, "What did you get, Slim?"

"Yesterday I got six hundred sixteen. Today I got six hundred seventeen. I don't know where the extra one come from." The difference in the numbers bothered me; I could count pretty good.

"I got six hundred fifteen," said Phil. "If I remember right, we turned out six hundred twenty-two last fall."

"I did find three cows dead during the winter and had two die tryin' to calve," I said.

"That's close enough," said Phil. "We've got

too much going on to worry about a missing cow or two."

I was surprised at Phil's attitude. He acted like he had plenty of cows and money. A missing cow or two would make most ranchers start out a search party. Cows meant money, even in poor years.

"What all's goin' on here?" I asked. "This looks like a county fair parkin' lot rather than a ranch."

"These are the neighbors and some relatives come to help brand," replied Phil. "They come every year and every year there seems to be a few more of them."

Trying to be funny, I asked, "Do you charge admission?"

Phil grinned. "No, but I ought to. I bet there's fifteen or twenty families here and probably ten or twelve hired hands from the other ranches in the county, along with a whole passel of kids. I used to feed them all, but there got to be too many, so I welcomed everyone that brought their own food, thinking that might thin a few of them out. A few didn't show, but more came in their place. I'm sure glad the hands brought their own horses and horse feed. The neighbors have made this sort of a spring get together the last few years."

"There's goin' to be a lot of confusion around the brandin' fire when we get to brandin'," I said.

"There'll be more than one branding fire," said Phil. "Last year we had three fires going. We might get four this year, depending on how many ropers we have."

"This whole deal might turn out to be more fun than a county fair," I said.

"We'll be pretty busy tomorrow. Tonight we'll have a meeting and see how many ropers we have and how many we have to be the ground crews. I kinda thought that you, Mike, Frank, and Angelo might be one crew. Mike can hold the calves down, Angelo can earmark, vaccinate, and castrate, and Frank can brand. You'll get plenty of practice roping."

"My ropin' could use plenty of practice," I said.

"The way I got it figured, you'll have about a hundred head of calves to rope, if we get four fires going," said Phil.

"What are all the kids goin' to do?" I asked.

"I'll have some of them hauling wood to each of the fires with a four-wheeler. Others will carry drinking water around to each one of the ground crews. You'll need to watch out for them when you're dragging calves up to your fire. Two years ago we had a kid get tangled with a rope when a feller was dragging a calf to the fire. Dragged him right off the four-wheeler. I thought he'd lost his head during the deal, but he wasn't hurt. The roper lost his calf. I've warned all the parents to watch their kids. I really get nervous during this deal."

"I'm goin' to get my bedroll an' figure out a place to sleep," I said.

"Angelo parked the trailer and set up a sort of lean-to toward the center of this holding pasture. He's fixing up some supper."

"I'll find him," I said.

"You might just as well go over there and relax some. There won't be anything to do until tomorrow."

I found Angelo and got my bedroll. I tried to find a level place to put my bedroll, free from rocks. I found a spot and stretched out.

"Angelo!" I hollered. "If I fall asleep, come over and give me a good, swift, hard kick when supper's ready!"

"It will be a pleasure, Señor," he replied.

I didn't know if he was serious or joking, but he was smiling when he said it. It wasn't long before I was asleep and it seemed even shorter when Angelo was kicking me, but not very hard. I woke up, still tired.

"Supper is ready, mi amigo! Come and get it before it burns up!"

Frank and Mike were already eating. I got a plate and dished up a steak, fried taters, and a salad. We hadn't had any salad up to this point.

"Where'd you get the fixin's for the salad?" I asked.

"Señor Phil brought them today," replied Angelo.

Presently Phil showed up and got his supper. While he was eating, between mouthfuls he said, "I've checked with everyone here and we have enough hands to make four fires to brand. Some of the crews will have two ropers. We should have this branding done in three days, maybe quicker."

"Then what?" asked Mike.

"Then we can get back to work when this playing is done," replied Phil.

"Where are we goin' to hold this gargantuan brandin'?" I asked.

"Right here in this holding pasture," answered Phil. "You'll notice everyone has set up their camps in the center. The cattle will pretty much be on the outside of the camps. We'll have the fires going toward the corners of the pasture and you won't have to drag the calves very far."

"How will you know how many calves get branded?" asked Mike.

"Each crew will keep the ears of the calves in a pile. When we're done we'll count the ears in each pile," replied Mike.

"We're going to cut off the ears of each calf?" queried Mike.

It was quite evident Mike was pretty green.

Phil grinned. "We're not going to cut off the ears completely. My earmark is an under-slope in the right ear. My brand is on the left ribs. They'll be marked on two sides."

Phil had Angelo, Frank, and Mike throw off the hay that was on the trailer.

"Make sure you leave enough hay on the trailer to feed the horses," I hollered at Frank as they left.

He had another truck loaded with hay on the outside of the pasture for feeding the next day.

I took my horses down to the creek, gave them a good drink and tied them to the trailer when Angelo returned. My horses were taken care of, I'd had my supper, and there wasn't anything else to do other than hit the sack. Phil, Angelo,

Frank, and Mike went and visited with the various cowboys and families. I was invited, but I didn't know anybody there and thought a good night's sleep would be more than welcome. I was asleep before the sun went down.

7

I was up early the next morning, even before Angelo. He'd been assigned the cooking chores, but I went ahead and started a fire and made coffee. I wasn't the first one up that morning. I could see folks getting fires started at their camps. I watched the sun coming up as I waited for the coffee to boil.

It wasn't long before Angelo was up. "Coffee's about ready, Señor," I said.

"Gracias," replied Angelo. He poured himself a cup and gestured toward me. "You ready?" he asked.

"Nope, I still got plenty. Looks like a nice day startin'."

"Si. You be plenty busy today."

"Looks like they'll be plenty of help," I replied.

"Si. This place will be like a, how you say? A circus?"

"I can imagine. It might be interestin' to watch."

"Watch? No, Señor. You get to be part of it!"

Angelo started fixing breakfast and I watched as the camp woke up. I finished my coffee and led my two horses to water. I gave them both a long drink then took them back to the trailer, tied them and gave them more hay.

Frank and Mike were up and eating their breakfast when I got back. I got some breakfast and watched the camp. Things were starting to happen. Fires were built toward the corners of the holding pasture, branding irons were put in the fires to heat up, and knives were being sharpened. Horses were saddled and ropes were taken down and shaken out.

I was saddling Diamond as Phil walked by. "Better get going, Slim, some of the boys have already caught calves and are dragging them to the fires," he said as he passed.

"Do we have our irons hot?" I asked.

"We're ready for you, if you can catch one," said Frank, grinning.

"That might be the hardest part of this job," I said.

I untracked Diamond, climbed on him, built a loop with my rope and rode into the cattle. I missed my first throw and looked back at Frank and Mike, waiting at the fire for me to drag a calf to them. They were both grinning and I imagined them saying something to the effect that they were going to have a pretty easy day at this rate.

My second loop was more successful than the first. I caught a calf, but only by one hind leg. I dragged him to the fire and Frank showed Mike how to hold the calf down by putting his weight on the calf's neck and folding a front leg back toward him. Frank then took the rope off the one hind leg and put both hind feet into the loop. I backed Diamond up until the rope was tight. The calf was stretched out on the ground and secured as long as Mike kept his weight on the calf's neck and the front leg folded back.

Angelo was already at work. He'd earmarked the calf and was castrating him. He'd give him a vaccination shot for Blackleg.

As Frank went to get the irons to brand the calf, he said to me, grinning, "We sorta prefer that both hind legs be caught."

I knew he was trying to tease me about only having caught one hind leg. "I'll try to do better," I said. "But it was so cold last winter, my rope is still froze!"

Frank laughed, got the irons and branded the calf. When he was done, he signaled to Mike to turn the calf loose and I gave the rope some slack. The calf got up, stepped out of the loop and trotted back to the herd.

I coiled my rope and went into the herd to catch another calf. I was successful again, only better. This time I caught both hind legs!

I dragged the calf to the fire and Frank said, "That's the way we like them!" as he helped Mike roll the calf over on his right side.

I roped for another hour or so. I lost track of how many misses I made or how many catches. I'd be able to tell how many catches I made when Phil counted the ears at the end of the day. I figured it was about even.

I was met with some irritating but humorous comments by Frank when I'd drag a calf up to the fire. On one occasion he said, "You're sure giving Mike and me plenty of rest time! We're not being over-worked!"

Another time he said, "Holler when you catch one and wake me up! I'd hate for Mike and Angelo to have to do all the work."

I was getting tired and when I dragged another calf to the fire, before Frank could make another remark, I asked, "One of you guys want to rope a few?"

There was no answer, so I asked, "How 'bout you, Frank?"

"Nope," was Frank's reply. Then he added, "You ain't taking my remarks serious are you? I was just joking."

"No," I said. "But I'm gettin' a little tired. I'm makin' a lot of throws, but only catchin' 'bout half of 'em. How 'bout you, Mike?"

"No." Mike's reply was short and kinda curt. I wondered if he was still saddle sore from the last few days or if he was working hard keeping the calves down while Frank and Angelo did all the work, branding, and castrating, ear marking, and vaccinating.

I asked Angelo if he wanted to try.

"Si Señor. I would give it a try," was his answer.

When they finished with the calf they were working on, I turned him loose, got off Diamond, and gave him the reins. Angelo got on and as I watched him ride into the herd coiling his rope, I said, "Don't be puttin' no kinks in my rope!" I thought to myself, *He's done this more than once.*

It wasn't long before he dragged a calf back.

"Nice catch," I said, as he brought the calf to the fire.

"Luck, Señor."

It wasn't long before he brought another calf to the fire.

"You didn't tell me you were an expert," I said.

"No expert, Señor."

"I don't believe it," I said.

Angelo just grinned.

While Angelo was roping, it gave me a chance to watch the other teams. Some had two ropers and there were some female ropers. They appeared to be pretty good. There were four different fires going, including ours, and there was plenty of action at each one.

There was a youngster on a four-wheeler and a trailer bringing fresh firewood to each fire. He also had water on the trailer. It was a welcome relief when he came to our fire. The four-wheeler tended to spook some of the horses and the youngster driving it had to use caution approaching the various teams.

At one point something put a spook on one of the rope horses and he went to bucking. I didn't see what spooked the horse, although I suspected it was the four-wheeler. He bucked his rider off then went running through the herd. When he got into our area, Angelo roped him and gently slowed him down. When he stopped bucking and running, Angelo led him back to where a cowboy on foot was walking toward him. The reins were broken.

"You lose your horse, Señor?"

"Yeah," came the gruff reply.

"I found him, Señor," said Angelo as he handed the broken reins to the cowboy, grinning.

He took the rope off, handed it to Angelo, said "Thanks" and walked off, leading the horse.

After a time Angelo gave me my horse back. "Tired," he simply said.

"You certainly put on a nice display of ropin'," I said.

"It was nothing, Señor."

"Your average is a lot better than mine. You didn't miss many."

After a time, Phil came to our fire. "How are you boys doing?" he asked.

"Okay, I guess," answered Frank.

"There's only one thing slowin' down our progress," I said.

"What's that," asked Phil.

"My ropin'," I replied.

Phil looked at the pile of ears on the ground.

"You're doing all right," he said. Then he continued, "It's getting to be around noon. You can stop and get something to eat if you want. Rest. It'll give the cattle a chance to settle down. They've become kinda restless. Some of the other crews have already stopped."

I looked around. There wasn't much action at the other fires.

"But we haven't got a cook and nobody put anything on our fire to cook," said Frank.

"Come over to my trailer," said Phil. "The missus has cooked up a noon meal and there's plenty. It's ready now."

"We'll be right over," said Frank.

"I'll unsaddle my horse, then come over," I said. I planned on using Buster during the afternoon.

I rode Diamond over to the creek, let him drink, then unsaddled him, hobbled him and turned him loose. Buster wasn't far off, grazing. I caught him, took off the hobbles and tied him to the trailer where I'd left my saddle. Then I went to Phil's trailer to get something to eat.

I'd only met Phil's wife once, when I'd hired on. She was a typical ranch wife, just a little over weight, but still attractive.

"You remember Slim, don't you honey?" Phil

asked as I approached the trailer. "I hired him last February."

"Oh yes," replied Mrs. Bennett. "Sit down here and get something to eat. There's plenty."

I took off my hat and said, "Nice to see you again, Missus Bennett."

"Yes," said Mrs. Bennett. "Sit down there and get something to eat! I don't know why, but around you cowboys, I always have to repeat myself. I wonder if it's because you all have fallen off your horses and landed on your head. Made you hard of hearing!"

I did as I was told and sat down beside Frank, who was silently grinning. He had his hat on, but I felt uncomfortable sitting at Mrs. Bennett's table with my hat on and put it under my chair. They had two kids, both boys, and I judged them to be about ten or eleven and eight or nine. The oldest one was the youngster driving the four-wheeler. I hadn't seen the younger boy around and figured his mother was keeping a pretty close eye on him.

We ate in silence and soon returned to our branding. The fire had burned down and Frank said, "There's no need to tell you, but take your time catching the first one. The irons need time to get hot."

I wondered if this was a sly way of remarking how poor my roping was, but let it pass. While I'd gotten some rest during the noon meal, I was still tired. My arm felt like it was going to fall off. I thought to myself, *You don't have to worry 'bout me gettin' in a rush. I'm goin' to take my own sweet time!*

I roped the rest of the day and when we stopped, I felt like I was worn out. Angelo started fixing supper and I rode Buster to the creek, let him drink, then rode back to the wagon, unsaddled him, hobbled him, and turned him loose. Then I went to the wagon, stretched out on my bedroll and hollered to Angelo, "Holler at me when supper's ready!"

I fell asleep and it only seemed like a few minutes until I felt Mike kicking at my feet.

"Wha, what's happenin'?" I asked, not fully awake.

"Angelo wants you to come to supper," said Mike. "It's ready."

Reluctantly, I got up and went to the fire.

"Your supper is ready, Señor," said Angelo, as he handed me a plate. "Is not as good as Señora Phil's, but it is all I could make."

"Gracias," I said. I didn't know much Spanish, but tried to use it around Angelo as much as I could. I don't know why, but I did.

After I ate, I went back to my bedroll and laid down to relax. At one of the other camps, somebody had a guitar and was strumming it. The music was more than relaxing and I soon fell asleep. I don't know how long I slept, it seemed like only a few minutes, but Angelo was poking me, saying, "Wake up Señor and get in your bedroll to sleep!"

I woke up. It was very dark. The fire had burned down and it was quiet in all the other camps.

"Worse than a hospital," I told Angelo. "Gettin' woke up to go to sleep!"

"You will sleep better in your bedroll with boots off," replied Angelo.

"You're probably right," I said. "But I ain't thankin' you! With this kind of service, can I expect breakfast in bed in the mornin'?"

"Si, you can expect, but I don't think you will get!"

I took off my boots, undressed, and got in my bedroll. I laid there out in the open, looking up at the stars and finally fell asleep again.

8

I woke up the next morning with Angelo poking me.

"Your pokin' me is gettin' to be a bad habit, Angelo!" I said. "Is breakfast ready?"

"Si, Señor," replied Angelo. "Everyone has ate except you. We thought you was dead."

"I guess I was pretty tired. You guys been workin' me pretty hard."

I got up, got dressed, and went to the fire for breakfast. Frank and Mike were enjoying their second or third cup of coffee when I joined them.

"Been waitin' long?" I asked.

"Nope," said Mike. "Just since sunup."

I checked the sun and it hadn't been up all that long. I looked around at the other camps. Things were just starting to stir there. I hadn't overslept all that long.

"As soon as I eat an' water my horses, we can start," I said.

"Take your time," said Mike. "We ain't in that much of a rush."

"Glad you feel that way," I said. "With a full day of ropin' yesterday to practice, my ropin' should be better today an' I can keep you busier."

"I hope so," said Frank. "I got so much rest yesterday between calves, I didn't sleep good last night."

He said that with a smile and I knew he was joking. I thought it was good that we could joke and I felt it was better to joke about my poor roping than another subject that might be offensive to someone.

I watered Buster and Diamond, grained them and got my own breakfast. When I was done, I saddled Diamond, shook down my rope and went to work roping calves.

I roped all morning and thought my roping had gotten better, although I wasn't keeping track of my catches and misses. Maybe it just seemed like I was catching more.

Along toward noon, I was getting a little tired and looking forward to a little rest.

Phil showed up and said, "Some of the guys

are telling me that the slick calves are getting a little scarce in the herd. How are you doing?"

"Okay, I guess," I replied. "There are still a few unbranded calves out there."

"When you're satisfied that they're all branded, give me a sign and I'll go around and start counting ears. Right now, dinner is almost ready at my camp. All you boys are welcome to join us, if you want."

"Of course we want," said Mike. "Angelo's cooking ain't bad, but it's getting a little old."

"Señor, you can do the cooking any time you want," answered Angelo, somewhat irritated.

"I'm getting a little tired of Mexican," said Mike. "My insides feel like they're burning up. And I think I'm getting the runs."

"If you prefer, you cook Italian or Chinese or whatever you want, Señor," said Angelo, even more irritated.

"I prefer good old American," retorted Mike.

I sat on my horse watching and listening to the goings on. I was halfway amused, but noticed a little animosity that hadn't been there before. But, I reasoned, it had been a long winter—cold and miserable. Then too, Mike had spent a few days horseback and he wasn't used to that. I didn't think my roping had improved enough that the guys were getting overly tired. I thought that everyone was looking forward to a few days off.

Phil noticed the apparent building up of animosity and said, "Dinner will be ready in about half an hour. You guys can knock off now and get ready for dinner if you want. It'll be American, Sloppy Joes."

"Good," said Mike. "I'm ready!"

I watered both horses and went to the noon meal.

During dinner, I asked Phil, "How do you figure things are goin'?

"Well, Slim, I think it's gone pretty fair. We haven't had any serious wrecks, other than that guy losing his horse yesterday."

"That wasn't too serious," I said.

"It could have been worse. I'm glad it wasn't," replied Phil.

"What you got planned when this is done?" I asked.

"We'll move these cattle up on the mountain tomorrow and turn 'em loose."

"Another day horseback!?" exclaimed Mike.

"Not for you," said Phil. "A few of these hands will hang around and help push the cattle onto the forest. You and I will go back to the calving

91

grounds after we count the cows out and bring the truck back to the ranch. It'll take all day for the herd to reach the forest and I'll meet you at the gate. We'll truck the horses back to the ranch. Angelo can take the tractor and trailer back to the ranch. Then, we'll take a few days off, go to town, relax some and take it easy."

"What you got for me?" asked Frank.

"Nothing really," replied Phil. "You can help move cattle if you want or head into the ranch, if we have enough help with the cattle."

"We'll see what it looks like in the morning," said Frank.

I could see that Frank wasn't too enthusiastic about another day horseback, but he appeared willing. Riding horses wasn't his thing.

"Slim, you can take off as long as you want," said Phil. "But I do need you back to start riding them four colts. They've all been halter broke, but that's all. I want them gentled so that my wife and the kids can ride them when they're ready."

"That'll take some doin'," I said. "But I don't need much time in town, just enough to get some new clothes, do laundry an' maybe sleep in a little."

"Whatever you want," replied Phil.

After the noon meal, we went back to branding calves. It wasn't too long before I was convinced that all the calves had been branded. I rode over to Phil and said, "I think they've all been captured and marked."

"Good," said Phil. "I'll get a couple of gunny sacks and start counting ears."

"Why the gunny sacks?" asked Mike.

"That's just so I can keep track of what I've counted," answered Phil.

Phil gathered up a few gunny sacks and with his oldest boy to hold the sacks open, he went to each fire and started counting ears. I watched as he went from fire to fire counting ears as he put them into the sacks. I thought it was kinda humorous to see him on his knees putting ears into the sacks, one at a time. When he finished at each fire, he'd mark the number of ears he counted in his tally book.

I decided we were done for the day and unsaddled my horse and turned him loose. When I had done that, Phil was counting ears at our fire.

When he was done counting our ears, he said, "You guys have roped and branded eighty-two calves in two days. Not bad! Another team that had two ropers didn't get that many. Of course, other teams that had two or three ropers did better."

"How many calves total?" asked Frank.

"I'm figuring that now," said Phil, totaling his tally book. "If my figures are correct, we have five hundred forty-seven calves. That's a fair average from over six hundred head, considering we're calving out on the range. The average might have been less if you hadn't been here, Slim."

The next morning, I was up early. I'd been told it would be a long day moving the herd to the spring and summer range. Angelo was already up fixing breakfast.

"You eat big this morning, Señor. It will be long day. I make you a few sandwiches to eat," he said.

"Thanks, Angelo. What are your plans when we're done here?"

"I go home to Mexico and visit my family. I will have the money Señor Phil owes me. We will be very rich."

"If you don't spend it before you get home," I said jokingly.

"No, Señor. I am not like Señor Frank."

"Señor Frank?"

"Si Señor. When he go to town, he always come home broke. He drink too much."

I ate breakfast, letting Angelo's comment about Frank slip by. I grained and saddled Buster. When I was through, I went back to the fire. Frank and Mike were eating and Phil had shown up.

"It looks like we'll have plenty of help to take the cows to the mountain," said Phil. "Take them slow. Let them graze along the way. It should take all day. I'll take Frank and Mike back to get the truck. Angelo can take the tractor and trailer to the ranch."

"Can you take my bedroll an' put it in the bunkhouse, Angelo?" I asked.

"Si Señor."

"I'm ready," I said, taking the sandwiches Angelo handed me.

"As soon as the other hands are ready, you can get started," said Phil.

Phil called for the other help to get started and they gathered around him as he gave instructions.

"Slim here will be in charge," he said. "He'll lead the herd up the creek until he comes to the water trough. Let the cattle water and rest there for about an hour or so, then head due south. About four o'clock, you'll hit the forest service gate. Just keep going. About a mile inside the forest property there's another water trough. Hold the herd there, let the calves mother up, then we'll be done. I want to thank all you folks for showing up and helping out. We'll be doing it again next year and you're all invited back. I've given instructions to those people who are going to take your trucks and trailers to the forest. They'll meet you there. Once again, thanks again."

I got on Buster and got ready to leave. Before I left, Frank came up to say so long.

"I won't be at the ranch when you get there," he said. "But I'll see you in a few days."

"Yeah," I said, wondering what Frank had in mind. No doubt he was going to town for a few days.

9

I got on Buster. Some of the volunteer help had already started pushing cattle toward the gate. Phil opened the gate and I went outside to get a final count on the cattle. I was busy counting cattle and didn't see Phil, Frank, and Mike leave.

When I was done counting, I ended up with six hundred seventeen, the same number I had when I'd counted them the second time. Satisfied, I went to the lead of the herd, telling all the riders along the way to take it slow and easy. The cattle were in a rush, they knew where they were going. I got in front of the leaders and slowed them down a little. The idea was to keep as many calves as we could with their mothers. When a calf gets separated from his mom, he'll generally go back to where he last sucked and look for his mom. The cow will generally do the same at feeding time.

We didn't have much trouble keeping the herd moving, although we had to slow the leaders down quite often. The two fellers Phil had assigned to help me were good hands and they made my job easier.

A little after noon, we came to the water trough Phil had mentioned. We held up the herd there and let them all water. I went back to the tail end to help push the stragglers.

When they were pretty close to the water trough, I said, "Keep 'em here, boys, an' don't let any calves go back."

"What about us women?" someone asked.

I hadn't noticed, but there were a couple of women helping the riders on the tail end.

"Where did you come from? I guess you can help the boys," I answered, somewhat taken aback. The women had bandannas around their noses and I hadn't really noticed them.

"We've been here since the start, a couple of days ago," answered one if the ladies.

"What are you doin' ridin' drag in all the dust?" I asked.

"This is where Phil told us to ride. Contrary to what a lot of you men think, we can do the work of a man," answered one of the women.

The gal seemed kinda cantankerous, and I

thought it best to let the situation rest where it was.

"You can go to the water trough one at a time to let your horses drink. Just don't let any of them calves or cows start back," I said.

I left and made a circle around the herd, telling everyone to let the cattle spread out a little and graze. Then I went to a high spot where I could see the whole area and started to eat the sandwiches Angelo had fixed for me.

As I ate, I watched the herd. A cow or two tried to go back, but the hands turned them back in the right direction and they were contained.

We spent about an hour and a half at the water tank. It was longer than Phil wanted, but I figured all the calves were mothered up. I made another circle around the herd, telling the hands it was time to go. I reminded them to go slow and went up to the leaders. After the water and rest, the cattle were ready to move and we had a little bit of a tough time holding them back. I was glad Phil had selected two good hands to help me.

Along about five o'clock, we reached the forest boundary. There were some trucks and trailers inside the fence, but I didn't see anything of Phil.

One of the people waiting inside the boundary said, "You're running a little late!"

"Yeah," I replied. "We let 'em rest a little longer at the waterin' tank."

"Well, I need to gather up my hands and go home. I've still got work to do there."

"That's fine," I answered. "We pretty well got 'em now."

When all the cattle had made it through the gate, the feller got his two hands that were on the tail end of the herd, loaded their horses in the trailer and left. I rode back to the drag to give the other riders some help. The two women were the only ones there.

"Can you gals use some help?" I asked.

"I think we've got them. The two guys that left weren't much help anyways," replied one of the gals.

"I'll give you a hand," I said. "We're almost done. We'll have to mother 'em up at the water trough, but as slow as we been goin', that shouldn't take too long. Most all the cows still got their calves."

"Many hands make light work," replied one of the gals.

I fell in behind the herd. I looked over the gals and their horses. The horses had been worked pretty hard and had worked up a good sweat. They were covered in dust pretty thick. They had more dust on them than the other two hand's horses had.

About a half a mile inside the forest, Phil showed up driving a truck, pulling a gooseneck trailer. He stopped to visit as he came up.

"I figured you'd be at the water trough by now," he said.

"We mothered 'em up at the last waterin' hole," I replied. "I didn't think it would hurt nothin'."

"That's all right," said Phil. "I'm running a little late myself. I had to pay Frank, Mike, and Angelo."

"What was Frank's rush to get to town?" I asked.

"He couldn't wait to start drinking. He'll be on a three or four day drunk, then it'll take him three days to sober up before he can work again."

"You put up with that?" I asked.

"Sure," answered Phil. "Frank's good help when he's not drinking. Last time he went to town, I had to get him out of the hospital, he'd drank so much. The doc said he almost died. Time before that, I had to bail him out of jail."

"Why put up with that?"

"He's good help when he's sober. There's nothing he can't or won't do and he's kinda like family. He knows he's got a job here as long as he stays off the bottle."

I let the matter drop.

"By the way," said Phil. "Angelo said to tell you he put your bedroll in the bunkhouse on an empty bunk. He also said to tell you adios and he hopes to see you in the fall."

"He's comin' back in the fall?"

"Yep. He comes back every year for the winter."

"What happened to Mike?"

"He went to town with Frank. I don't know if he'll be back," answered Phil. "I told him we could use him in the hay this summer."

"We'll have to mother up the herd when we get to the water trough," I said. "Shouldn't take too long, we brought 'em plenty slow."

"I'll just follow along," said Phil.

We pushed the stragglers to the water, then waited until the calves all found their mothers. Some of the hands loaded up their horses and left. Soon it was just the two gals and the two fellers that helped me at the head of the herd. I found out that the gals were married to the two guys.

The gals made an interesting picture when they took off their bandannas. Their foreheads were covered with dust and there was a definite line where their bandannas were. The area covered by the bandannas was fairly clean, although the bandannas didn't keep all the dust off. As soon as possible, the gals went to the water trough to wash up. But they didn't make it before their husbands came riding up to them.

All of the sudden, I heard a big laugh coming from the water trough. The husbands had seen the women before they got the dust off and were giving them a big hoorah.

"Just go ahead and laugh, Mister Bill! Next time I'll ride up front and you can follow the cattle. We'll see how clean you are after following six hundred cows and their calves ten or twelve miles up a dry trail."

It was quite apparent the gals didn't see the humor in the situation and I had a hard time to keep from laughing when I saw the gals.

"You always wear lipstick on a cattle drive, darling?" asked Mister Bill.

"Only to prevent chapped lips," replied his wife.

"Even with all that dust on you, you still look pretty good to me," said Mister Bill, trying to worm his way out of a situation that could only get worse.

His partner, seeing how things were going, didn't say anything. But he did offer his wild rag to his wife to dry off her face.

Watching and listening to what was happening, I asked Phil, "Are them folks always that formal, what with the Mister Bill?"

"No," answered Phil. "Janet's just a little upset."

I continued to watch the situation. Presently, Janet asked, "Well, Mister Bill, aren't you going to offer me a dry wild rag to wipe my face with like your brother did for his wife?"

"Sure, darling," said Bill, riding his horse over to his wife. He reached into his pocket, pulled out his wild rag and leaned over offering the wild rag to Janet.

Janet, rather than reaching for the wild rag, grabbed Bill's outstretched hand and pulled him out of the saddle and into the water trough!

Bill was taken totally by surprise and would have drowned if the water had been more than two and a half feet deep! Bill struggled to get to his feet and Janet said, "Now we can all laugh at something!"

Everyone was laughing and I had to join

them. Even Bill was laughing when he got to his feet.

"Well, darling," said Bill, "we're even. You can stop that 'Mister Bill' stuff. Come over here and help me get out of this thing!"

"Not on your life, Bill! I know you too well and I don't want to end up in that trough myself!"

Bill just laughed as he stepped out of the water trough. "Now darling, come over here and help me get dried off."

"Not while you're that close to the water trough," retorted Janet.

Phil, the other couple, and myself were laughing pretty hard.

"If that's what married life is like, I'm glad I'm single," I said.

"They're really very happily married," said Phil. "But there is a little of the devil in each one of them."

"They can keep it," I said. "I think we need to stick around here for another half hour or so just to make sure the calves have all mothered up."

"We can load up whenever you're ready," replied Phil.

"Where's Janet an' Bill's truck?" I asked.

"They're going to ride back in our truck. There's enough room in the trailer for their horses. The girls can ride up front with me and you three guys can ride in the back. It shouldn't be too tough."

"Whatever," I said.

Shortly, confident that everything had mothered up, we loaded the horses and headed out. When we got to the forest gate, I got out and opened it. After Phil drove through it, I closed it. I wanted to make sure it was closed properly, just in case some of the calves hadn't found their mothers.

On the way to the ranch, I found out that Bill's brother was named Jerry and his wife's name was Pam.

When we got to the ranch, we unloaded the horses, unsaddled and grained them and turned them loose. I was shown where the bunkhouse was and found my bedroll. I had some clean clothes stuffed in between the bedding and mattress. I thought a shower and some clean clothes would be just the thing. Before I got into the shower, Phil came to the bunkhouse.

"The missus and I would be real pleased if you'd take your meal with us," he said. "Bill and Jerry and their wives will be joining us for supper and you're invited. It will be ready in about half an hour."

"Just enough time to get a shower," I said. "Will it be safe with Janet there?"

Phil laughed. "She promised me she'd be on her best behavior for supper. I've lent Bill some clothes while his are being washed and dried. They'll all stay here tonight and I'll take them back to get their truck tomorrow."

"I'll be there just as soon as I get out of the shower," I said.

"Good! Don't forget to get dressed before you come!"

I decided while I was in the shower that this was a pretty good outfit. It seemed like Phil could see the humor in just about anything.

At supper, Bill and I were the only ones with clean clothes on. We were taking some ribbing from everyone else because we did have clean clothes. When Phil mentioned that I was the only one that had really cleaned up because I'd had a shower, I became the butt of their merciless ribbing.

"It appears that we have a real gentleman amongst us tonight," said Janet.

"Not really," I said. "Bill has had the benefit of a bath already today thanks to you and the water trough. I'll admit I did have the benefit of soap! And I'm not sure I'd have needed a shower if I'd have been closer to you and that water trough!"

Everyone laughed and we had an enjoyable supper, with only a little bantering between all of us.

After supper, I excused myself and started toward the bunkhouse. Phil stopped me and asked, "What are your plans for tomorrow and the next few days?"

"I expect I'll go to town, do some shoppin' an' be back tomorrow night," I said.

"You're not going to get drunk?" asked Phil.

"No," I answered. "I want to look at the colts you've got for me to break an' I'd prefer to have a clear head doin' that."

"Good," said Phil. "Come to the house for breakfast, about six, and I'll write you a check for your wages."

"I'll see you at six," I said and went to the bunkhouse.

The next morning, I went for breakfast. Phil already had a check written out.

"You can cash that at the bank," he said. "It's good. If you see Frank, try to talk him into coming back early."

"I don't think I'll see him as I'm not figurin' on goin' to jail or the hospital," I said.

I took the check, thanked him and went to my car. I thought I'd need to jump-start it because it had set so long without being run, but it started right up.

It was about fifty miles to town and on the way, I made a mental note of what I needed. Clothes, jeans, shirts, underwear, socks, long johns, a little of everything. I thought I might sort through what clothes I had, and maybe throw away some of the older well-worn items and do laundry with the rest. I had enough money to completely outfit myself with plenty, but decided not to splurge.

I cashed the check and went to a western wear store. I think they were glad to see me leave. I didn't cause a problem, but I left with four pairs of jeans, half a dozen shirts, plenty of underwear, long johns and socks. It all amounted to a pretty sizeable bill and when I did leave, they invited me back! No wonder.

It was early afternoon when I left the store. I decided a big steak dinner was in order, so I found a steak house and had an early supper. After supper, I was ready for a nap, but decided to return to the ranch and hit the sack early.

It was almost dark when I got to the ranch. Phil was just finishing up his nightly chores when I drove up.

"You didn't spend much time in town," he said as I got out of the car.

"Nope," I replied. "Towns don't hold much interest for me. I think they were glad to see me leave."

"Glad to see you leave? Did you get into trouble?" asked Phil.

"Nope," I answered. "But I did leave a lot of money before I left. They even invited me back!"

Phil laughed. "I see. You want to look over the colts you're supposed to break?"

"It's gettin' dark. Let's do it in the mornin'."

"Fine," said Phil. "After breakfast."

The next morning it was raining and raining pretty hard. I got my slicker from my saddle and went to the big house for breakfast.

At the table, Phil said, "These colts have been halter broke but that's about all. They've never been saddled or rode. I need them broke real good so that the missus and the kids can ride them safely."

"That will take a little time," I said.

"We have plenty of time, all summer if you want, even into the fall. I just need a good job done on them. The missus doesn't want me breaking any horses since Buster broke my leg. And the bloodlines indicate there's some buck in these horses. I think they're all three years old."

We went to the corrals to look over the colts. They were all big and stout. There were two bays, a palomino, and a sorrel paint. And they were fat and in good shape.

As we approached the corral the colts came up to the fence as if to greet us. I think they were looking for their breakfast.

As Phil threw them some hay, he said, "The wife wants the palomino for her to ride. She thinks he's pretty. The two bays are for the boys and I thought I'd ride the paint."

"He ain't much of a paint, just one white spot on his flank," I said.

"All he needs is one spot, bigger than four inches, to be a registered paint," said Phil.

"Are all these colts papered?" I asked.

"Yep." replied Phil. "The paint is registered. The palomino is registered with the Palomino horse registry and the two bays are registered Quarter Horses. We went a little wild at a horse sale we went to about a year ago. I was going to start riding them as two-year-olds, but the missus didn't like that idea and I got kinda busy and didn't have the time. You know, most all my help quit me last spring right when we were ready to start irrigating. Frank and Mike were all that was left. Then I hired those two drifters that I fired last winter. Angelo showed up and Bill and Jerry showed up occasionally to help out in the hay. It's been a pretty rough year."

"Sounds like this is a cooperative operation," I said.

"Well, we do get a lot of help from the neighbors."

I went to the gate and let myself into the corral. I walked among the colts and they didn't show any fear or try to get away. I opened the gate to the round corral and let the colts in.

"You got four halters an' lead ropes?" I asked.

"Yep," answered Phil. "They're in the barn. There's also some old saddles and bridles in there."

"I'll get the halters," I said. "Might just as well get started right now."

"You don't waste much time, do you," said Phil.

"Nope," I said as I left the corral and went to the barn. I returned with the halters and a curry comb and a brush. I caught each horse and tied him to the fence, then went to brushing each horse. While they all seemed gentle enough, I thought a lot of ground work wouldn't hurt anything, especially me!

When I finished brushing each one, I picked up their feet. The paint and palomino stood good when I picked up their front feet, but resisted strongly when I tried to pick up their hind feet. The palomino pulled back and fell sideways when I tried to pick up his left rear foot.

"Well, Little Outlaw," I told him. "Looks like we'll have to do some considerable work on your hind end."

I always talk to the horses I'm either breaking or riding. It seems to calm them some. This was no exception. I kept working on picking up his rear foot and finally got him to yield it to me. When I got it picked up, I set it back down real easy.

"That's enough, Little Outlaw. We'll continue tomorrow," I said. "Your education ain't complete yet!"

I picked up the paint's hind feet, and while he resisted, he didn't raise a ruckus like the palomino.

I continued talking to the horses as I worked.

The two bays didn't resist at all when I picked up their feet.

I hadn't noticed, but Phil showed up while I was busy. He didn't say anything until I decided to take a little breather.

"Starting right from the beginning, huh?"

Startled, I answered, "Yep."

"What do you think so far?" asked Phil.

"They seem gentle enough. I brushed 'em all over an' they just stood for it. I didn't have no trouble pickin' up the two bays' feet. The paint resisted some, but not much. The palomino pulled back an' threw himself the first time I tried to pick up his left rear. I've got a sneakin' hunch he's probably a barn-raised colt an' when someone tried to pick up his hind feet, he raised a ruckus, they got scared an' quit. But I managed to pick up his foot."

"Did you get kicked?"

"No," I answered. "If you know how to do it, you can keep from gettin' kicked most of the time. We'll do plenty of ground work before we start ridin' 'em. Makes the first ride easier."

"You do what you need to do."

"Those old saddles in the barn, can I use 'em?" I asked.

"Sure," replied Phil.

"I'll get 'em an' we'll continue these horses' education."

"I'll help you bring them over," said Phil.

We went to the barn and I carefully checked the condition of the cinches and latigos on each saddle. When everything passed inspection, I took two saddles and Phil took two back to the corral.

"I'll saddle each horse an' let him stand for a bit. We'll let 'em get used to a saddle on their back. We better get some saddle blankets so we can sack 'em out."

"What's this 'we' stuff?" asked Phil. "I'm not involved!"

I laughed. "I guess I mean me when I say we. Comes from livin' alone too much an' havin' conversations with myself. Gets really difficult when I get into arguments. I never can tell who won."

Phil was laughing at my explanation as we walked back to the barn to get saddle blankets. We got four pads and four blankets and took them back to the corral and dropped them in front of each horse. The two bays didn't react and I suspected they'd been sacked out before. The paint pulled back, as did the palomino.

The paint stepped forward but eyed the blankets suspiciously. The palomino continued to pull back. He acted like the blankets were a dangerous enemy. I was hoping the halter and lead rope wouldn't break.

"This palomino is goin' to take a little more time," I told Phil. "I don't know what you call him, but I've named him Little Outlaw."

"The missus won't like that," said Phil laughing. "She was going to name him Cupid or something like that, I can't remember."

"Hopefully Cupid will fit him when we're done with him. Course, some outfits name all their tough horses with names like that, or flowers or somethin' not really fittin' the true nature of the horse."

I started to sack out Little Outlaw. I was flopping and waving the blanket all around him. He raised the dickens and it took quite a while before he decided the saddle blanket wasn't going to hurt him. It would take a few more sessions of this same treatment before he got used to it.

I was busy and didn't see Phil leave.

As I sacked out the palomino, I kept an eye on the paint and the two bays. The paint spooked, but didn't spook as badly as the Little Outlaw. The two bays just stepped away, but watched what was happening. From the palomino's reaction to the sacking out, I figured it would take some time to get him used to it. But, Phil had said we had plenty of time.

I gave each one of the other colts the same treatment I'd given Little Outlaw, but didn't get the same reaction.

Then, I saddled each one of the colts. It was plain that they'd never been saddled before and it was a struggle with each one to get the saddle on. After I saddled each colt, I moved the saddle back and forth on each one of the colts. I wanted them to get used to some movement on their backs.

Little Outlaw threw himself again when I tried cinching him up. When he got up, I cinched the saddle. Now that all the colts were saddled, I thought I'd let them stand, saddled, just to get used to the saddle on their back. I thought I ought to saddle a horse and lead each colt around, but decided against it. A few days of sacking out and saddling each colt then letting them stand wouldn't hurt anything.

I was taking a break, watching the colts, when Phil returned.

"Are you going to work right through the noon hour?" Phil asked.

"I hadn't figured on it. What time is it?"

"It's past noon. The missus has been keeping your meal hot."

"I better go eat," I said. "I don't want to get on the wrong side of your missus. These colts can stand where they are. The palomino's still fightin' a little, but he should be all right."

Dinner was on the table when I got to the kitchen.

"What do you think of my palomino horse?" asked Phil's wife.

Not wanting to be put on the spot, but trying to be honest, I answered, "He's all right. He's got a little more fight in him than the others."

"Don't let him hurt himself," said Phil's wife.

"He has thrown himself a couple of times," I said. "He scraped himself up some, but he'll be all right. He's pretty good at spookin' the other horses. What do you call him?"

"Golden Boy."

"Oh," I said.

"What do you call him?" asked Phil's wife.

"Well, from his actions, I've started callin' him Little Outlaw," I replied.

"Oh, my goodness! Is he a bad horse?"

"I don't think he's a bad horse. He just don't know nothin'. He's got a lot to learn," I said.

Then, trying to keep the situation from getting worse, I added, "You know, the old timers used to say 'If there ain't no buck or fight in a horse, he ain't no good.' That's probably true. With some time and a lot of ridin', he should be okay."

Phil's wife seemed to accept my explanation and I ate my noon meal in relative quiet. I never did talk much while I was eating.

After dinner, I went back to the corral. I decided to lead each one of the colts around on foot in the corral before I turned them loose. They were all a little hesitant when we started, taking tentative steps to begin with. They'd never walked with a saddle on their backs before and didn't know what to expect.

The two bays accepted the situation and after a time were following me freely. After I'd led each one around, I unsaddled him and turned him loose in the corral where they spent their days. The paint took a little more time but was soon walking, following me freely. Little Outlaw was a different situation.

As soon as I asked him to walk, he started bucking. I let go of the lead rope and climbed up on the fence where I could watch the action and not get in the way or get hurt. The palomino did a good job of bucking. He fell once and I couldn't tell if he'd slipped or threw himself on purpose.

When he tired and stopped bucking, I went to him, got the lead rope and asked him to walk again. Once again, he started to buck, but it wasn't as hard or ferocious as the first time. This time I held onto the lead rope and soon had him bucking and running around me in a circle. When he stopped, I unsaddled him and turned him loose in the bigger pen with the other colts. I threw them some hay and sat on the fence watching them eat.

"Today's been a pretty bust day for all of us," I said. "But we'll repeat it tomorrow and for a few days after that. The more ground work we do, the better off we'll be."

As I sat there, I reflected on the day's activities. I concluded that the palomino would be the main problem, the paint would present some problems, and the two bays would be the least of my problems. I decided that I'd follow the same course of action for the next few days as I'd done today.

Phil approached while I was sitting on the fence.

"How'd it go today?" he asked.

"Pretty good," I replied. "We've started their

education. How come you always show up when I'm not doin' anythin'?"

"I have been watching you periodically. I didn't want to come over while you were working. The yellow horse did a pretty good job of bucking, didn't he."

Phil's comment was more like a statement than a question.

"Yeah," I answered. "I think some rodeo stock contractors would be interested in him to use in their buckin' horse strings." I told him how I'd rated each colt based on today's actions and responses. He seemed to agree.

10

I followed the same procedure for the next four days. All the colts seemed to settle down and accept the sacking out process except the palomino. He didn't fight as much but he did still fight the process. I did think I could see some improvement in his attitude.

Sometime during this period, Frank showed up. He came to the corral the next day and didn't look good. He had a bad hangover. I didn't say anything as he watched and eventually he said, "If you need any help, give me a holler."

I decided I wouldn't need any help until at least he felt better.

On the fifth day, after I'd saddled each colt, I decided to saddle Buster and lead each colt around outside the round corral. We could move faster and the stirrups bouncing around and hit-ting the colts on the side would be good for their education.

Buster had a little hump in his back when I saddled him. He hadn't been rode for a week or so. I untracked him and had him trot around me in a circle until he relaxed. Then, expecting the worst, I climbed aboard. I sat there a moment, shifting my weight in the saddle back and forth. He didn't do anything and when I cued him, he walked right out.

I rode into the round corral and untied one of the bays without getting off Buster. The colt followed willingly and we headed out into the hay fields and we got into a trot. As I rode, I tried to think of some names for the two bays and the paint. One bay had white socks on two of his feet. Socks would be a good name for him. I didn't know what to call the other bay, but thought I'd watch his personality and name him accordingly. I decided to call the paint One Spot, as that's all he had.

We didn't have any trouble until we came to an irrigation ditch full of water. Buster jumped the ditch, but Socks hesitated. When he refused to jump the ditch, he almost pulled Buster backward, but Buster regained his balance and remained upright. I'd had the lead rope dallied loosely around the saddle horn, and when Socks pulled back, it took all the slack from the lead rope. I almost lost it.

We were at a standoff, Buster and I on one side of the ditch, Socks on the other. The lead rope was tight between us. We were in a predicament.

I turned Buster to face Socks. Socks had been good to lead and I tried to figure why he balked at the ditch. I finally came to the conclusion he balked because he didn't know what the ditch contained or how deep it was. I'd been told that horses don't have any depth perception in their vision. I don't know if that's true or not, a horse never told me that.

I backed Buster up a step or two, almost dragging Socks into the ditch. He jumped it, banging into Buster on the other side of the ditch. Buster spooked and jumped backward when Socks hit him and I almost fell off.

After Socks hit Buster, he took another jump, but we held him. When he stopped, I saw him warily eying the ditch.

"It's okay, Socks. It won't hurt you," I said, as I scratched him between the ears.

Having got over the ditch once, I decided to

cross it again. Repeating lessons often is how a horse learns.

"We'll do it again, Socks," I said to the horse. "Repeatin' is how a horse learns. Come to think of it, that's how a person learns too! Maybe there ain't that much difference between us!"

We crossed the ditch again and this time Socks didn't resist as much. A couple of more crossings and I was sure Socks had overcome his fear of the water in the ditch.

I continued to ride leading Socks for about another hour. When I got back to the corrals, I gave Buster a rest, let him get a drink, then got the other bay and led him out into the hay fields. When we got to the irrigation ditch, having been through the trouble with Socks earlier, I was better prepared for crossing the ditch with this colt. But the colt crossed the ditch willingly, just pausing long enough to assure himself that the ditch and water didn't pose a threat to him.

Just to make sure that this crossing wasn't a fluke, we crossed the ditch a few more times, without any trouble.

I rode for another hour or so and didn't have any problems and returned to the corrals. I unsaddled Buster and turned him loose. It was time for the noon meal.

At dinner, Phil's wife asked, "When are you going to start riding the colts? I would like to come and watch."

"It'll be some time yet," I answered. "There's still a lot of ground work to be done. Little Outlaw will probably …"

"Golden Boy you mean," interrupted the woman.

"Whatever," I continued. "He'll probably be the toughest. I want to make sure they don't buck. If they start buckin' an' decide they like it, it might be tough to get that idea out of their heads."

Phil's wife appeared to accept my conclusion and didn't ask any more questions.

After dinner, I saddled Diamond, got the paint colt and led him out of the corral. When we got out in the open, the paint wanted to run, but I had him dallied up pretty tight and maintained control. We hit a trot and kept it up until we got to the irrigation ditch. We stopped there to let the paint assess the situation.

Dallying up pretty tight, Diamond jumped the ditch and dragged the paint with him. The paint almost went down in the ditch, but I kept his head up and he regained his balance. A few more crossings and One Spot was crossing willingly. He was getting the idea, as were the others.

An hour later, we returned to the corrals. I got Little Outlaw and started to lead him out of the corral. I expected some trouble, but the colt followed Diamond freely. When we hit a trot, Little Outlaw kicked up his heels, but didn't try to buck. I'd left the yellow colt until the last, expecting him to give me trouble. Of the four colts, I trusted him the least.

All the colts were responding well to my instructions, however Little Outlaw still resisted to some of the training procedures. He still was reluctant to give me his feet when I went to pick them up, but he was slowly yielding.

When we got to the ditch, the palomino jumped it willingly after Diamond. I'd expected trouble and wasn't disappointed when it didn't come. Little Outlaw seemed to be a follower.

After a trip outside the corral with each one of the colts, I decided it was time to start getting the colts ready to be ridden. The next day I saddled One Spot, put a hackamore on him and started having him go around me in a circle. We did this at a walk, then I urged him into a trot. I'd slam the bosal down on his nose, step in front of him and say "Whoa!" at the same time. This action would cause him to stop.

Then I'd approach him and pat him on the

neck as a sort of a reward. I'd then start him in the opposite direction and repeat the procedure, rewarding him with a pat on the neck and some soft soothing language at the same time.

I repeated the procedure with all the colts, spending forty-five minutes to an hour with each one. I didn't have any real trouble with any of the colts. After a few days of this, I started to hold onto the saddle horn and raise myself up a little. This put my weight on the saddle. Both bays accepted this, but One Spot and Little Outlaw tried to jump away from my weight as I lifted myself from the ground. Both of these colts would need more work doing this before I actually got into the saddle.

I did this again for a few days on both sides of the horses. For some reason or other, a horse needs to be taught the same lessons on each side. They can't reason that what's done on the left side is applicable on the right side. They need to be taught.

Content that the two bay colts were ready to be rode, I decided it was time to get on. I saddled Socks, ran him around me in a circle, both ways, put a little weight on the saddle, then took hold of the headstall (cheeking), put my left foot in the stirrup, pulled his head toward me and swung into the saddle, saying "Whoa, Socks." Once in the saddle, I turned his head loose. He eyed me warily for a second, but just stood there. I shifted my weight back and forth in the saddle.

I nudged him lightly in the ribs with my spurs and he took a hesitant step forward. I nudged him again, gently, and he moved forward a little less hesitantly. He didn't know what was expected of him.

"You're gettin' the idea, Socks," I said as we walked around the corral. "Now let's see if you can turn."

I pulled his head around to the left and although he resisted some, he decided to turn and follow his head.

"Good!" I told him. We did a few more turns to the left and then we turned to the right. The colt was moving more freely.

I rode the colt for about fifteen minutes then decided to call it a day with Socks. Short but frequent training sessions work best with young horses.

I stopped the colt and stepped off. When I got on the ground, Socks jumped away from me, spooked, like he'd forgot I was around.

"Well, Socks, this ain't goin' to do. We'll have to extend this trainin' period some."

I got on him again and without asking him to walk out, got back off. He jumped away again, only this time not as far or as frightened. I got on and off him another eight or ten times until he stood still when I dismounted. The last time I got off, I patted him on the neck, told him he was a good horse and turned him loose.

As I let him go, I said, "Don't you think too much about today's lesson an' decide you don't like it. We've got to do it again tomorrow."

I got the other bay colt, saddled him, and got on. He didn't do anything when I got on. He didn't want to move when I nudged him with my spurs so I used my spurs a little harder. He jumped forward, but stopped.

"At least that's movement," I said. "Let's see if we can get you walkin'."

I used the spurs on him a little harder and he jumped again. This time he didn't stop and took another jump. I wasn't surprised and was ready for it. Before he stopped, I used my spurs again and he jumped again. He wasn't really bucking, just jumping like he was jumping the irrigation ditch.

I kept this up until he quit jumping and started walking.

"That's some improvement," I said, as we

walked around the corral, hesitantly. "Now let's see if you can turn." I pulled his head around and he turned to the left. A few more turns to the left and we turned to the right. The colt responded.

I got off and the young horse just stood there. I thought it would be a good idea to get on and off a few more times before I turned him loose and did it.

Then I caught One Spot and saddled him. He was still a little spooky and I decided to do more ground work before I got on him. I knew that it was easier to break and train a horse if I could keep him from bucking and the more ground work I did with the horse, the easier he would be to train.

I messed with the colt for about an hour and turned him loose. Then I caught Little Outlaw, saddled him and repeated the same lessons we'd went through previously.

The next day I repeated the same lessons with all the colts. I rode the two bays in the round corral and even got them into a slow lope. I got on and off each colt a number of times and nothing unexpected happened. The two bays were learning their lessons well.

One Spot and Little Outlaw were still quite

wary of me and what we were doing. I continued the ground work and decided I'd keep it up until both colts learned to trust me a little more. It was slow, boring work, but I knew it must be done in order to make good horses out of them. However, the colts were responding, it was just taking them a little more time. Like Phil had said, we had plenty of time.

After about a week of riding the two bay colts in the round corral, I took them into a larger corral and rode them each for about an hour. They were responding well, turning in each direction and stopping. It was about time to take them outside.

I thought One Spot and Little Outlaw were improving and decided they needed to be ridden. I saddled One Spot, did all the ground work I'd done before and got ready to get on him. I cheeked him, put my left foot in the stirrup, grabbed the saddle horn and started to swing up. At this movement, the colt moved away from me, but I had his head and pulled him in a circle around me. I still had my foot in the stirrup and was hopping around on one foot, trying to stay with the horse. Finally, my foot slipped out of the stirrup, I stopped hopping on one foot, and the colt stopped trying to get away from me.

Another try and I made it into the saddle, although when I got in the saddle the colt was in the middle of a jump. I still had a hold of the headstall with my left hand and a hold of the saddle horn with my right hand. I let his head go, but still held onto the saddle horn. This wasn't the time to do any fancy bronc riding. If the colt bucked me off, he might think he could do it any time and he'd be harder to train. If he decided he liked to buck, it would be tougher.

I let him buck in the round corral until he tired. I was getting tired, too. When he finally quit bucking, he started running. I let him run until he tired, then encouraged him to run some more. He was breathing hard when I finally pulled him up and let him stop. I sat on the horse and shifted my weight sideways in the saddle. The horse simply stood there, breathing hard and eyeing me as if to say "What do you want me to do now?"

I got off the horse. I was a little winded, too. I decided now would be a good time to get on and off a number of times while the horse was tired and not so apt to try and get away. I got on and off a number of times and One Spot was content to let me do it without trying to get away.

"I hope you've learned your lesson, youngster,"

I said. "That buckin' is hard work on you an' it ain't easy on me. I hope you'll learn that it's easier to cooperate than fight!"

I got on him again and rode him around the corral, pulling his head around in each direction I wanted to turn him. Being tired, he responded easily. He stopped when I pulled the mecate on the hackamore and said "Whoa!"

Pleased with his actions, I unsaddled him and turned him loose. I then caught Little Outlaw and repeated all the ground work we'd been through before. It was time to get on and ride him.

I cheeked him, put a foot in the stirrup and swung up in the saddle. I was a little surprised that the colt didn't try to jump away when I mounted. I'd expected the worst from this colt as he was the slowest to respond to any of the training. I sat there, shifting my weight back and forth in the saddle. The colt just stood there, not knowing what to expect.

I touched him gingerly with a spur and felt him tense up under the saddle. *Here it comes,* I thought. I readied myself in the saddle, and touched him again. He didn't try to buck or jump, but took a step forward. Surprised, I encouraged him again and he started to walk out. He was unsure of himself, but he walked forward.

I let him walk, not trying to direct him. I stopped him and decided to get on and off for a time. I did this without any fight from the horse. The last time I got on, I rode the horse around the corral, turning him in both directions and stopping him frequently. Teaching a horse how to stop is very important. Pleased, but surprised at the colt's reactions, I unsaddled him and turned him loose.

Phil had walked up to the round corral as I was riding the yellow colt. "How's he coming?" he asked.

"He seems to be comin' along okay," I said when I'd turned the colt loose. "The paint colt had more buck in him earlier today. I expected more fight from this horse."

"You want them to fight?"

"Certainly not," I answered. "But this palomino colt sorta surprised me today. He might think about it tonight and put up a struggle tomorrow. We'll see."

"I think the wife will want to come out and watch you tomorrow," said Phil. "Do you mind?"

"I don't suppose so," I answered. "However, I don't want her doin' anythin' that will spook any of the colts."

"I'm sure she won't," replied Phil.

The next morning, I saddled each one of the bay colts and rode them in the bigger corral. Each colt was a little unsure of himself, not knowing what to expect, but I didn't have any trouble. Each colt responded well to the turning and stopping, remembering yesterday's lessons. I got on and off a number of times with each colt. I was satisfied.

Then I saddled One Spot and he once again tried to get away as I swung into the saddle. He started to buck as I rode him in the round corral. The colt didn't buck as hard as he did the day before and he stopped when I stopped him. After his little foolishness was over, I walked him around, turning him in each direction and stopping him quite often. I got off and on a number of times until the colt stopped trying to get away.

I hadn't noticed but Mrs. Bennett showed up while I was getting on another time. "Did he buck you off?" she asked.

Startled, I replied, "Nope." Then, seeing who it was, I added, "This is just part of their training."

"Are you going to ride Golden Boy?"

"Yep," I answered. I decided I was not going to get into an argument about the horse's name—Golden Boy or Little Outlaw.

"When?"

"Just as soon as I've finished with this colt," I answered. "He's needin' some additional ridin'."

Phil's wife climbed on the fence. I was about to say something as the colt spooked, but decided her actions would just be part of the colt's training. It might be good to get the colt used to other people being around.

When I'd ridden One Spot about forty-five minutes or an hour, I unsaddled him and put him in his pen. Then I caught Little Outlaw and saddled him.

"Is this the horse you wanted to watch me ride?" I asked jokingly. Of course, I knew it was.

"Yes," replied Mrs. Bennett, missing the poor attempt at humor.

I got on the horse and he just stood there. When I touched him with a spur, he jumped forward and Mrs. Bennett yelled, "Come on Golden Boy!"

At Mrs. Bennett's yelling, the horse jumped forward again, but it was only a halfhearted jump. I got him to trotting around the corral.

Then I said, directing my comment to Phil's wife, "You know, Missus Bennett, you're not supposed to root for the horse!"

"But he's my horse!"

"True," I said. "But you don't want him buckin' every time he hears a different sound when you're ridin' him, do you?"

"Certainly not!"

"If you'll get down off the fence an' open the gate, I'll ride him out in the big corral an' we'll see what he does."

Mrs. Bennett jumped down from the fence and almost fell when she hit the ground. The colt spooked at this action, but I soon calmed him. When the gate was open, I rode the colt into the larger pen. The colt was a little hesitant to go into the larger area, but I encouraged him with a spur. Unsure of what was going to happen, the colt entered the big pen. I rode him around in the pen and he soon relaxed. I had him walking, trotting, and even got him into a slow lope in the big pen.

We went back to the round corral and I unsaddled the colt.

"Are you done already?" asked Mrs. Bennett.

"Yep," I answered.

"It doesn't seem like you've done much with him today," she said.

"Yep," I answered. "Short training sessions are best. A horse remembers what he's been taught better that way than tryin' to cram a lot into his head all at once. Look at what slow trainin' has already done."

I picked up each one of the horse's feet without him bein' tied to the fence. I rubbed him all over and walked behind him. Mrs. Bennett was unimpressed. She didn't know that a colt has to be taught all these things.

Phil showed up. "What do you think of your horse's training?" he asked.

"He's certainly taking his time," replied Mrs. Bennett.

"Well, Slim knows what he's doing. I think he's done a terrific job, so far," said Phil.

"But I want to ride my horse," said Mrs. Bennett.

"It'll be quite a while before you ride this horse," I chimed in. "I don't fully trust him yet. I've got an idea he's goin' to surprise me at some point."

Mrs. Bennett didn't say anything, but I knew she was thinking that she "loved the horse and the horse would return the love." I also knew that this was a foolish thought at this stage of the colt's training.

11

The next few days went about the same. I spent a lot of time riding all four colts in the big pen, then decided to take them out in the hay fields. I saddled the unnamed bay colt and prepared to ride outside the pens. Matt, Phil's oldest son, showed up and was watching. I figured he was ten or eleven years old.

"What do you call that horse?" he asked.

"I haven't really named him yet," I said. Then deciding to have a little fun with the boy, I added. "Both him an' the other bay look exactly the same."

"No they don't!" retorted the boy.

"They don't?" I questioned.

"No! The other one has white feet!"

"He does?" I tried to muster up as much surprise as I could. "Well, I'll be darned. He does! What would you name him?"

"I'd call him White Feet," replied the boy.

"How's 'bout Socks?" I suggested. "It's 'bout the same thing."

"You can call him whatever you want. I'll call him White Feet," said the youngster.

"What would you call the other one, No Feet?"

"No," replied the youngster. "He has feet. I'd call him Bay Boy."

"Well, you just named him," I said. "Bay Boy it is."

While we were talking, I got on the horse. I didn't expect him to do anything and he didn't.

"If you'll open the gate, I'll ride outside," I said. "Stand back out of the way. This colt ain't used to seein' little people."

Matt looked at me. "I ain't little," he muttered.

The boy opened the gate and the horse walked out, looking all around as if this was new scenery. It was new territory for him to be ridden in. As we went farther from the corrals, I could feel him relax. *This is a good thing,* I thought.

I rode to the irrigation ditch and the colt only hesitated a little before we jumped it. I halfway expected the colt to take another jump when he jumped the ditch, but he didn't.

"All that repetition jumpin' the ditch before

has paid off, Bay Horse," I said. "Oh, excuse me! Bay Boy is the name Matt gave you."

I laughed at my mistake and the thought that the horse would take offense at it.

We made a big circle around the hay field and stayed out about two hours, then showed up at the corrals. I thought that maybe I'd stayed out too long, but the colt didn't seem tired.

Matt came out from the house when I returned. "Did he buck you off?" he asked.

"Nope," I said, as I got off and started to unsaddle the colt. "Why do you ask?"

"My dad said I get to ride him when he's ready. I told Dad that I'd already named him."

"Yep." I said. "An' he already knows his name. Call him an' see if he knows it."

As Matt called "Bay Boy, Bay Boy," I gently pulled the horse's head in Matt's direction, hoping the boy wouldn't see.

He didn't see and was really pleased that the horse responded to his new name. "You'll be the best horse in the whole world," he said. He reached out and petted the horse on the nose.

"Yep. He's done very well today."

"When can I ride him?"

"It'll be some time," I said. "We need to make sure he remembers the lessons I've taught him.

These young horses tend to forget easily, just like you youngsters."

"I don't forget nothing!" said Matt emphatically.

"Now he gets to go rest an' think about what we've done today while he's eatin'." I turned the colt loose and caught Socks.

"You going to ride that horse today?" asked Matt.

"Yep, your horse ain't the only one that needs an education." I thought that Matt had a lot of questions and decided he was getting a good education. About what, I wasn't sure.

I saddled Socks and got on to ride him outside. We went pretty much the same way as I did with Bay Boy. When we got to the ditch, Socks hesitated and I had to encourage him with the spurs. He finally jumped the ditch and took another jump when he got to the other side.

"That's enough of that foolishness," I said, as I pulled his head up. He didn't jump anymore. We stayed out about as long as I did with the other horse.

When I got back to the corral, I found Matt in the corral with Bay Boy, telling him what a good horse he was going to be. When I saw that, I was thankful I'd spent a lot of time doing all the ground work with the colt.

Phil showed up and was surprised to see his boy in with the colts. "You get out of there right now!" he commanded. "Don't you know you could get hurt?"

Matt left the corral and said to his dad, "That horse won't hurt me. He's mine and I'm going to make him the best horse in the world!"

"All them colts are really gentle," I said. "I spent plenty of time on the ground around 'em. I won't guarantee it at this point, but he should be all right in there."

"That boy doesn't know enough to be in among those young horses at his age," said Phil.

"You'll probably have a tough time keepin' him out from now on."

"You can help the boy's education by letting him come watch you and telling him what you're doing while you're doing it."

"I could do that," I said, "But only if the boy minds me."

"Oh, I'll mind you Mister Slim. You bet!"

Phil nodded his head approvingly.

"Course, you know," I said, "there's an extra charge for educatin' the boy. I really only hired on to educate the colts. Boys are harder to educate."

Phil laughed. "You might be right," he said.

I told Matt to sit on the fence while I caught and saddled One Spot.

"Aren't you going to get something to eat?" asked Phil.

"Don't have time. I'm puttin' about two hours worth of ridin' on each one of these colts an' I don't want to be late for supper."

"He don't need to eat, Dad," said Matt. "He's a cowboy. He's tough."

I rode One Spot out of the corral, laughing at Matt's comment. We made the usual trip out to the irrigation ditch. The paint colt put up quite a fight, but I finally got him to cross it. We made a few more crossings and kept it up until the colt didn't fight as much. I wasn't satisfied, but returned to the corral knowing I still had to ride Little Outlaw. I decided that tomorrow I wouldn't spend as much time riding the bays and spend more time riding One Spot over the ditch. I needed to get him so he'd cross the ditch without resisting at all.

Back at the corral, I unsaddled One Spot and saddled Little Outlaw. I didn't expect any trouble from the colt and when we got to the ditch he crossed it easily.

I made it back to the ranch and turned the colt loose in time for supper. I looked forward to

Mrs. Bennett's cooking. It was a lot better than mine or Angelo's.

At supper, I asked Phil, "You got anythin' that needs doin' horseback? I'm getting' kinda bored just ridin' around the hay fields an' I'd kinda like to show the colts some new country."

"There are some yearlings in what we call the sand dunes out south. It wouldn't hurt to ride through them and see how they're doing."

"Tell me how to get there an' I'll head out tomorrow morning," I said. "All them colts could use some extra miles." Phil gave me directions.

The next morning I saddled Bay Boy and made ready to go out and look at the yearlings. Matt was there and had plenty of questions. I left, leaving most of Matt's questions unanswered.

I rode through the hay field until I came to a gate. I got off the colt, opened the gate, got back on and rode through the sagebrush. I'd left the gate open because Phil had said there were two gates and I knew I'd be coming back. I'd close the first gate when I came back through it on the way home.

I kinda let Bay Boy wind his own way through the sagebrush. I'd neck rein him around some of the brush. He stumbled a time or two as I wanted him to go one way and he'd start to go the other. Going through the sagebrush this way reinforced his neck reining. And I also cued him with a spur on the opposite side of the way we were going.

When I got to the second gate, I got off, opened it, led Bay Boy through it, closed it and got back on. It wasn't long before I spotted a bunch of yearlings trailing to water. I counted them and followed them to the water hole. I'd counted fifty-three. There were supposed to be about a hundred head here. I still had forty-seven head to find.

I made a circle around toward the east, looking for the other yearlings, but without finding any. Judging by the sun, I figured I'd been out about three hours. I started heading back toward the ranch. I didn't want to over work Bay Boy.

I got back to the ranch about an hour later. Phil met me at the corral.

"I saw 'bout half the yearlin's," I said. "Is there another water hole out there?"

"Yes," answered Phil. "It's about four or five miles to the west."

"I'll change horses an' go back to look for the other yearlin's," I said, as I unsaddled Bay Boy and caught Socks.

I saddled Socks and headed out again.

Knowing I had another four or five miles to ride, I hit an easy trot until I got outside the first gate. In the sagebrush, I let Socks walk, working on his neck reining as I'd done with Bay Boy.

I got to the second gate, opened it, led Socks through it, closed it and headed off in a south-westerly direction. There wasn't any need to go to the water hole I'd been to before, as I'd already seen the cattle there. I figured I'd save some time and miles taking the angle to the second water hole.

There were some yearlings at the second wa-ter hole, I counted about thirty head. I still had twenty-some yearlings to account for. I'd seen most of the yearlings and made a circle back to the northwest, heading toward the ranch and looking for more yearlings. As I rode through the sagebrush, I thought I'd give Bay Boy and Socks tomorrow off and use Little Outlaw and One Spot. As the colts improved, I thought I could ride them longer when their turn came and give them some rest time.

I got back to the ranch in time for supper. I unsaddled Socks, fed the colts, and went to feed myself.

"You didn't ride Golden Boy today," said Mrs. Bennett.

"Nope," I said. "His turn is comin' tomorrow. I've been ridin' each colt for about two hours a day. Today, the two bay colts each got about four hours worth of ridin' an' tomorrow each one of the other colts will get about four hours. They're all comin' along pretty good an' some extra rest time shouldn't hurt 'em none."

Mrs. Bennett didn't say anything.

I told Phil, "I've accounted for around eighty head of yearlin's. I've still got twenty or so to find. I'll go out tomorrow an' look for 'em. The ride will do the other two colts a whole lot of good."

The next morning, as I was saddling One Spot, Bill and Jerry, Phil's neighbors, showed up. We visited for a time then Jerry asked, "How are you coming with the colts you've been riding?"

"Good," I said. "This here is one of 'em. He's 'bout to go out for about four hours. What are you doin' here?" I said as I got on.

"Phil's about ready to start cutting hay. We came over to help. You got the colts pretty well broke?" asked Bill.

"They're comin' along," I said, as Bill took his hat off and threw it at One Spot's feet. The colt jumped backward, but didn't buck. He eyed the hat on the ground suspiciously.

"That's pretty good," said Bill as he picked up his hat.

"Just part of the trainin'," I said as nonchalantly as I could. Bill's action had spooked the colt some and me even more. Secretly, I was pleased that the colt hadn't blown up. I also thought I'd better keep an eye on Bill. He might cause some real trouble around the colts in the future.

I headed out to see if I could find the other yearlings. I thought, as I rode, that this year was passing quickly. It was already hay-cutting time. I hadn't paid much attention to the date as I'd been working the colts. I did notice it was getting warmer and I'd shed my long johns some time ago.

I got to the first gate, opened it and left it open. At the second gate, I noticed some cattle off in the distance. After I entered the area, I closed the gate and went toward the cattle. I made a big circle, counting cattle as I went. Before I started back toward the ranch, I'd counted ninety-four head. *Almost all of 'em,* I thought. I figured I'd saddle Little Outlaw and come out this afternoon and look for the rest.

The ride back to the ranch was uneventful. I switched horses and headed back to where the yearlings were pastured. It might prove difficult to see all hundred head during the same day. I thought maybe I'd better ride around the fence and check it. I wasn't familiar with the country and this would help me get to know it better.

At the second gate, I headed due west, keeping an eye on the fence and an eye looking for cattle. Little Outlaw had a fast, easy walk and we covered the ground quickly. About a mile and a half from the gate, I found a dead yearling. I figured it had been dead about two weeks or so. The carcass was pretty well chewed up and I couldn't tell what had killed the critter.

As I rode, I noticed some larkspur growing among the sagebrush. *That yearling probably died from larkspur poisoning,* I thought. Phil wouldn't be too happy that one of his yearlings was dead.

I rode farther and came across another dead yearling. I thought both critters had been dead about the same amount of time. I saw more larkspur.

"Well," I told Little Outlaw, "that's two less yearlings that we have to account for. However, that don't shorten our day, we've still got to cover a lot of ground."

It was well after dark when I got back to the ranch. I met Phil and Frank in the hay field. They were in the pickup.

"I was headed out to look for you," Phil said. "I was getting kinda worried, it's late. Did you have any trouble?"

"No trouble," I said. "Just a long ride. I made it almost all the way around the fence, but it got dark, so I headed toward home. I did find two dead yearlings. I couldn't tell what killed 'em, but I'm guessing it was larkspur poisonin'. What's Frank doin' with you? It seems like I haven't seen him all summer."

"Frank has been irrigating, he was concerned so he came along. Larkspur poisoning? We've never had any problems with that before."

"I'm just guessin'," I said. "I did see a lot of it. I'm told cattle can eat the leafy part without any harm. But when the ground is soft and they pull up the roots an' eat 'em, that's where the poison is. It was hard to tell. The coyotes had pretty well cleaned 'em up."

"It did rain a couple of weeks ago," said Phil. "Maybe that's when they died."

"I don't know. It looked like they'd been dead a couple of weeks."

"What can you do to cure it?" asked Phil.

"I'm told when you see a cow that's been poisoned, you cut her tail off an' let her bleed out," I said. "I've done it a number of times an' it seems to work."

"Oh really?" questioned Phil.

"Yep," I said. "I had to cut off about twenty tails workin' for one rancher." Then, deciding to have a little fun, I added, "That rancher was really mad at me even though I'd saved his cows."

"How come?" asked Phil.

"He told me that when he sold the cows, he had to sell 'em wholesale."

"Wholesale? How come?"

"He told me he had to sell 'em wholesale because he couldn't retail 'em!"

Phil laughed. "You do have a wry sense of humor, Slim. Sometimes I don't know how to take you. Let's head back to the ranch. The missus has kept supper for you."

"You go ahead. I'll follow," I said.

"Don't you want to use the lights of my truck?" asked Phil.

"That might be an idea, but Little Outlaw can see good enough."

"Go ahead, I'll follow," said Phil. "He can probably travel faster if he can see better where he's going."

I started out with Phil following in the truck.

But Little Outlaw was acting strange. He became kinda spooky, and I had a hard time keeping him lined out. Finally, I figured it out. The colt was afraid of his own shadow! Each time he moved to the right, his shadow also moved and he reacted. His reactions were becoming stronger. I finally moved off to the side and motioned Phil forward.

When he got even with me, I said, "You go ahead. I think the lights of the truck bother the horse."

"I saw he was acting strange," said Phil. "What's up?"

"I think he's afraid of his own shadow," I answered. "He'll travel better without the lights."

Phil drove the truck ahead of us and the colt moved out more freely. Content that I had identified the problem, I thought about how to solve it. The only solution I could come up with was to ride the horse after dark with the pickup lights shining the way, or ride the horse early in the morning when the shadows were long. I opted for the early morning rides. After riding for better than eight or nine hours a day, I was tired.

When I got to the ranch, I took care of the horse then went to the house to eat. Mrs. Bennett wasn't too upset that I'd returned late, in fact she inquired as to her horse.

"How did Golden Boy do today?" she asked.

"He got used more than four hours today," I said. "But I think he's a big chicken!"

Mrs. Bennett looked shocked. "A big chicken! What makes you say that?"

"Well, he's afraid of his own shadow!" I replied.

Mrs. Bennett didn't say anything and allowed me to eat my late supper in peace.

The next day, I saddled Socks and went out to look for the missing yearlings. Socks had a full day off and was feeling pretty good. I got to the second gate of the pasture where the yearlings were held and rather than going west as I had the day before, I went east. I thought I'd ride the fence in the opposite direction and stop when I got to the spot where I'd quit the day before.

I did come across another dead yearling and I figured she died from the same causes as the other two. I crossed a small stream and followed it to the west. Along the stream, I found five more yearlings. Content that I'd seen about all the yearlings, I went back to the fence and rode it until I came to where I'd stopped the day before.

The fence didn't need any repairs. I headed back to the ranch.

Going through the hay field, I came across Jerry cutting hay. Socks showed some interest in the swather, so I rode him over toward it to get him better acquainted with it. As we approached the swather, Jerry shut the machine off, indicating he wanted to visit.

"How's it going?" he asked when we approached.

"Okay," I answered as I took in the smell of fresh cut hay. "Smells good when it's fresh cut, don't it."

"Yep. It's the only benefit in a dirty, dusty job. I kinda wish I had a job like yours, just riding around horseback all day."

"Your job ain't much different, just ridin' around on a swather all day," I said.

"Yeah," answered Jerry. "But you don't have to put up with the dust and dirt."

"True," I responded. "Then again, you don't have to worry about the swather buckin' you off!"

Jerry laughed. "You're not worried about being bucked off, are you?"

"Not with the two bays. But I still don't trust the paint or the yeller colt a hundred percent."

We visited for a while, then when Jerry started the swather, Spot spooked and jumped sideways. I calmed him down and continued to the corrals.

"Looks like we'll have to get you used to bein' around machinery," I told the horse. I decided I'd ride each colt out around the farm machinery just to get them used to seeing and hearing it.

Having given Spot a full day of riding, I decided to give him a day off the next day. I could spend two or three hours the next few days riding the colts around the farm machinery, getting them used to the sounds of the moving equipment. Other than a lot of riding, a lot of miles, the colts were pretty well broke. They'd need more riding before I felt confident letting Phil's kids or his wife ride them.

I told Phil that it would be some time before the kids could ride the horses.

"That's okay," he said. "If all the colts need more riding, just keep doing it. I don't need anybody getting hurt."

"It would be a lot easier on me if we had a job to do with the colts rather than just riding around."

"You can always go up on the mountain and check the cattle up there," said Phil.

"That's more ridin' in a day than I want to

give the colts," I said. "Course I could take a packhorse an' some groceries an' my bedroll an' spend some time doin' it. You got a pack saddle?"

"I think there's one in the barn. I've never used it," replied Phil.

"Fine. I'll spend a few days leadin' the colts around together, then put together some groceries an' head out."

"Why do you want to lead all of them together?" asked Phil.

"Just so that they're used to it. It'll be a new, different experience for them."

The next day I saddled Bay Boy, tied the other three colts together at the halters and started out to watch the farm hands put up hay. I didn't want to use a head to tail tie for fear one of the colts might pull back and break another colt's tail.

Jerry was still cutting hay with the swather, Bill was baling hay, and Phil was loading hay with a bale wagon.

The baler made a lot of noise and the colts hesitated about getting too close to it. I was content to follow along, gradually shortening the distance between the baler and the horses as they became accustomed to the sound of the baler and the bales falling off the end.

The bale wagon was a neat piece of machinery. One man could drive it, load each bale, then the machine would place the bale in position on the wagon. When the driver had a full load, he'd drive to the stack yard, pull a switch and the machine would lift the load, put it upright, and slide out from under it. The driver didn't even have to get out of the cab to do all this.

As I watched, I couldn't help but think of all the time, growing up, that I walked alongside a wagon, throwing bales up on it. And throwing them pretty high. Someone else would stack it on the wagon. When we had a load, we'd all get on the wagon, ride to the stack yard and stack it. It was a lot of work and the most enjoyable part of it was the ride back and forth to the stack yard. Although I didn't think it was possible, someone had apparently detested haying more than I did to come up with such an ingenious invention!

The next day, I saddled Socks, put the pack saddle on Little Outlaw, tied the three colts at the halter and went out to the hay fields again. I put Little Outlaw in between Bay Boy and One Spot so they could get used to the pack saddle and pack bags bumping against them. That caused a little bit of a problem, but soon we were lined out in good order.

Each day, I rode a different colt and had a

different colt carrying the pack saddle. I changed the order in which I tied the colts together so they could get used to the pack bags bumping them on both sides.

The colts were getting used to the haying machinery, scarcely paying it any attention when we approached and followed it. I decided it was time to go on the mountain. That night, I got some canned goods that would be easy to cook, a spoon and fork, an axe, plenty of matches, and whatever else I figured I needed for a week's stay out on the mountain. I packed it in the pack bags and other than rolling up my bedroll and saddling up, I was ready to go the next morning.

The next morning, I was up early, as was everyone else. Phil, Bill, and Jerry had brought in the farm equipment for servicing. They needed greasing and oil changes.

I was saddled up, packed up and had the three colts tied together. I'd packed some grain to give to the horses each day. I figured it would help keep them close to camp.

I rode over to the shop to tell Phil about how long I'd be gone when Bill started the swather. It started with a big backfire and Little Outlaw, the colt I was riding, spooked and started bucking. I couldn't pull his head up and lost the lead rope to the other three colts. They ran, trying to buck as they ran.

Little Outlaw bucked and I couldn't get him stopped. He was really scared and was bucking through the unused farm equipment. His bucking was getting stronger. All the riding I'd put in on him had got him into shape and he wasn't tiring. He was bucking through the harrows, discs, plows, side delivery rakes and other equipment. I hoped he was watching what he was doing. If he stepped or fell on any of that equipment, he could seriously hurt or cripple himself!

Hurt himself! I thought. *If he bucked me off onto any of that equipment, I could get seriously hurt or even end up dead!* I got as good a seat as I could, and grabbed the saddle horn for insurance. This wasn't a time to be showing off any bronc riding skills! Trying to guide the horse out away from the farm equipment was out of the question.

As the horse bucked, I felt myself getting loosened up in the saddle. I was fearful that the colt would buck me off! The colt seemed to be gaining strength as he bucked! I envisioned myself bucked off, flying through the air and being impaled on one of the harrows or being sliced on one of the discs. I didn't like the thought of either action.

With all the strength I could muster, I grabbed the mecate with both hands and pulled as hard as I could. I pulled his head around but not up. He didn't stop bucking. He got out of the parked farm machinery and bucked right into the pole fence, slamming my right leg into the poles. I blew my right stirrup.

It was certain the colt wasn't watching what he was doing. The fence didn't stop his bucking and he turned back into the farm machinery, still bucking. Once again, I grabbed the saddle horn and tried to fish for my blown stirrup. In the middle of the farm equipment, I was wishing I'd have gotten off on the fence, but I didn't have time. His bucking action was coming too fast and it was quite furious. I had to ride the colt at least until he bucked out of the machinery or risk being hurt myself.

He finally bucked out of the machinery and with more room, started to run. I let him run and when he started to tire, I made him run more. When I finally stopped him, he was breathing hard. When the backfire scared him, he forgot all his training and was bucking out of fear.

I walked him back to where Phil, Bill, and Jerry were watching the event. When we stopped,

Little Outlaw was shaking all over. It had been quite a tiring experience for him.

"Quite a rodeo you put on!" said Phil.

"It was totally unplanned," I said. "Did you enjoy it?"

"It was quite a show," said Jerry. "Did you get hurt when he slammed you into the fence?"

"I don't think so," I replied, as I caught my breath. "But I can feel some pain in my leg."

"What set the horse off?" asked Phil.

"The backfire from the swather," I answered. "It's really tough to get 'em accustomed to everything, especially the unexpected. I never have completely trusted this colt. That's why I call him Little Outlaw."

Bill had caught the other horses. They hadn't gone far. He led them up to me and asked, "You still going up on the mountain?"

"Yep," I said. "I'm packed an' ready to go. Phil, can you tell me where there's a good place to camp? I've never been up there before."

Phil gave me instructions on where to find a spring on the mountain. I told him I'd be back in five, six, or seven days and not to worry. I headed out.

The ride up on the mountain was uneventful,

other than a sage hen flying up and spooking all the colts. Other than the colts jumping sideways, they didn't do anything. I was dallied up and didn't lose the colts I was leading.

I found the spring and made a camp. I would camp out in the open, under the stars. I'd eat out of the cans, heated in a fire. I had a pair of pliers to get the cans out of the fire. I figured I'd have a fairly comfortable camp, other than a slight throbbing in my right leg. I hobbled all the colts, gave them some grain to keep them close to camp and went to bed.

The next morning, I was up early. I made coffee and looked around. The horses were close to camp and I saddled One Spot for the day's ride. I would ride out, get accustomed to the country and look for cattle. It would be a welcome change from riding in the hay fields.

12

Riding through the aspen and pine trees was a nice change. The shade helped cool the day. I saw cattle all day long. They were well scattered. I didn't know it, but Phil had brought up a bunch of bulls earlier in the month and they were also well scattered. I didn't notice any salt and thought packing salt to the cattle would be a good job the rest of the summer, if there was a good camp set up. I made a mental note to mention it to Phil when I got back to the ranch.

I'd covered a lot of country, getting to know the lay of the land and One Spot had a good workout. Each day I used a different horse and they all had good workouts. I did come across a couple of deer carcasses. From the way they'd been covered, I figured a mountain lion had killed them.

On the fifth day, I saddled Little Outlaw, tied

the other three colts together and rode back to the ranch. I got there just in time for supper. While eating, after taking care of the horses, I told Phil about my plan to scatter salt on the mountain. I finished by saying, "If there was a good camp up there, I could spend a lot of time scattering salt an' looking after cattle. If the salt were scattered, it might help keep the cattle spread out. You got a tent an' a small cook stove?"

"No," answered Phil. "But that sounds like a good plan. If you want, you could go to town tomorrow and get the stuff you need to make a camp. Get some salt, too. There isn't any here."

"I'd need 'bout twenty blocks, half a ton," I said.

"Take the pickup," said Phil. "I'd go, but we're not done in the hay field. Bill's done cutting hay, he can go with you and help you load salt. There's a road up on the forest service land. It's farther to the south and off to the west. It's mostly used by the forest service and some hunters in the fall. You can charge the salt and stuff you need to my account."

I'd come across the road while riding on the forest and about midway up the mountain saw a place that might make a pretty fair camp. Being about halfways up the mountain, it might make a good base to scatter salt from.

"I saw the road," I said. "There's a fair place to camp halfways up."

The next day, Bill and I went to town. I had Bill drive, I kinda liked the idea of being chauffeured. Our first stop was at the barbershop. I was feeling a little ragged and needed a haircut. After a close haircut and feeling more human, we went to the hardware store. We loaded twenty blocks of salt in the front end of the truck, then went to look at tents.

I wanted a tent big enough that I could stand up in it and it needed a stovepipe opening in the top of it. I picked out a small stove and a cot. I also got a folding table and a kerosene lantern and kerosene. I got two folding chairs. I also got a tarp to cover the salt with.

"Why don't you get a chaise lounge?" asked Bill.

"What for?" I questioned.

"Then I'd have a comfortable place to park when I came to visit you," he replied.

"This is stuff I need to work with," I said. "This ain't no vacation!"

With all the items loaded, we headed back to

the ranch. On the way, Bill said, "We might just as well leave this stuff on the truck. I can drive it up tomorrow."

"Good," I answered. "We'll also need some grain for the horses and plenty of groceries for me, along with some pots, pans, an' utensils. We can get them from Missus Bennett."

The next morning, while I was saddling One Spot, Phil and Bill loaded groceries, cooking utensils and grain onto the truck. I put the pack saddle on Socks and put my bedroll on it. Then I tied the three colts together and rode over to where Phil was.

"I'm going with Bill to the mountain," he said. "I want to know where you're camped up there."

"That's fine," I said. "I'll see you up there."

I turned my horse to leave and Phil said, "There's a good place to camp up there and a spring close by. When you hit the forest service road, turn west and keep coming until you find us. We'll set up your camp and be waiting for you."

"Good! If you'd have the noon meal ready, that would be extra nice."

"The wife is sending up the noon meal with us," said Phil.

"That's even better!" I replied.

I rode for about four hours, found the forest service road and followed it. About an hour later, I came upon Phil and Bill at my camp. They'd set up the tent, gathered up some firewood and were sitting around waiting for me. Bill was sprawled out on a chaise lounge, halfways sleeping. Phil was sitting on one of the folding chairs.

I unsaddled the horses, hobbled them, gave them some grain and turned them loose. I put my bedroll inside the tent.

"Your dinner is ready," said Phil. "Bill and I already ate."

He handed me a plate, kept warm in the warmer in the stove.

"Careful! It's hot!"

It was hot, but I managed to set it on the table before I spilled any. As I ate, I asked Bill, "Where'd you get that?"

"What?" asked Bill

"That lounge chair," I replied.

"I put it in the truck when you weren't looking."

"It's here. You might just as well keep it," said Phil. "Just one of the comforts of home. I also brought a rifle. It's in the tent. You might want to try for the mountain lion you say is up here."

"I ain't goin' to pack a rifle around lookin' for a cougar," I said. "If he comes close to camp, I might try to get him, but I ain't huntin' him."

"How do you plan on distributing the salt?" asked Phil.

"I figured I'd put the salt up high on the ridges. The cattle can utilize the feed between the water an' the salt. Makes better use of the feed."

"Sounds good," said Phil. "We'd better be going, I'll be up in a week or so to bring you more groceries and check up on you."

"I'll be around, somewheres," I said.

I had forty blocks of salt to scatter. If I loaded four blocks on one of the colts each day, I had about ten days of salt scattering. Two hundred pounds shouldn't be too much for each one of the colts to carry. I didn't weigh near that and the extra weight should actually do the colts some good. As I rode, I began thinking of ways to extend my stay at the camp.

It was a good camp. It was cooler than down at the ranch and the water was good and cold. There was plenty of feed and the horses stayed close to camp.

I thought I could spend a few extra days just checking cattle and even only pack a hundred pounds of salt on some days. Of course, if it rained, I wouldn't even go out, I could spend the day in camp. I could spend a few days riding and fixing fence, although I hadn't noticed any spots where the fence needed immediate attention.

The colts were coming along good and the only one I didn't trust completely was the palomino. I thought he'd never be completely trustworthy, and should be a cowboy's horse.

When Phil showed up about a week later, I told him of my plans.

"That's a good idea," he said. "How come you want to stay up here?"

"It's cooler here than down at the ranch an' I've got a good camp. Besides, I thought I'd like to take more advantage of that chaise lounge that Bill left. I couldn't do that at the ranch."

Phil laughed. "You might look for that cougar while you're up here," he suggested.

"I haven't noticed any sign of him," I said. "Besides, I'm told they cover a pretty big range. He's probably long gone by now."

"It wouldn't hurt," said Phil, "seeing as you want to just kill time." Phil was smiling as he said that. "How are the colts coming?"

"They're all workin' out good. They'll all pack or ride. The two bays will probably be the best. They should be just fine for your boys. The paint is comin' along good but I still don't trust the palomino. He'll need a lot more ridin' before I'd let your wife ride him."

"Then get as much riding as you can on him. He needs to be plum gentle for my wife. What are you figuring on doing when we're done here?"

"I hadn't really given it any thought," I answered. "I'd like to go somewheres where it's warm for the winter."

"You know, we can always use you when we're calving," said Phil.

"I figure I'll be done here in about three weeks or a month," I said.

"You stretch it out as long as you want," said Phil. "The more riding those colts get, the better off they'll be. Maybe you can get the colts to working in a bit rather than a hackamore. I'd like to keep you around as long as possible, but we don't really have a fall gather. We just open the gates and the cattle work their own way down to the wintering grounds. There's some riding when we sort the calves from the cows and ship them, but that's about it."

"I'll figure on rollin' up in about a month. I don't know about calvin' next year, that's a long way off. But we'll see."

I hadn't really thought about what I was going to do when this job was over, but Phil made it clear there wasn't going to be much when I was done. I had a few options open. I could stay in the area and help with some other rancher's fall gather. I had the thought that I could go visit my brother, but he'd probably put a shovel in my hands and send me out irrigating. I didn't much care for that idea.

"I'll bring up some fencing equipment next time I come up," said Phil before he left.

I packed salt the next few days making sure the yellow colt carried two hundred pounds each time I used him. He was really getting a day off, kinda, when he carried my hundred and sixty pounds. I made sure the two bays only carried a hundred pounds when I used them. With the paint, I alternated between a hundred and two hundred pounds each time I used him.

One afternoon, I did take the rifle out a couple of hundred yards from camp. I'd noticed some deer in the area and thought some venison steaks might be a nice change in my diet. I sat in the shade and waited for the deer to come to water.

When they showed up, I shot a nice forked-horned buck. He was in good shape and I didn't waste any time cleaning him out. I skinned him and quartered him, then hung the quarters in the shade. I took the heart and liver and made supper out of them. The fried heart, liver, and potatoes made for a good meal that night.

The next morning, I wrapped the quartered deer in some extra blankets to keep in the coolness and keep the flies off and hung them in the trees. I dragged the head and hide a good distance from camp and halfway buried them. I hadn't seen any forest rangers but didn't want to take any chances and get arrested for poaching.

In the afternoon, the next few days, I came to camp early and cooked up some roasts thinking that I could use all the meat before it spoiled.

When Phil showed up again, he had some more groceries and some fencing tools. I began to regret volunteering for the fence fixing. I'd just about run out of salt and that was the only job that would keep me on the mountain.

Phil and I visited for a time and when he got ready to leave, I gave him a hind quarter of venison.

"You've been getting a little red meat, huh?"

"I was target practicing one day, just in case I did see that mountain lion and this deer just walked in front of one of my bullets. I couldn't let him lie an' go to waste, could I?" I responded.

Phil smiled. "No, I guess not."

The next day, I saddled One Spot, put a leather bag of staples, a bag of clips, and a hammer on the saddle and went to fix fence. I thought the fence fixing would go fairly well. I'd go along and just staple the top wire in the posts. I'd use the clips on the steel posts.

I went back to the road and was going to follow the fence to the east, when I noticed a truck coming up the road. I recognized the truck as a forest service vehicle. I waited at the gate and opened it for the ranger to come in.

"Howdy," I said after the ranger came through the gate and I closed it.

"Howdy," replied the ranger. "What are you doing up here?"

"I've been haulin' salt for Phil Bennett's cows, an' lookin' after them some. I'm figurin' on ridin' fence for the next couple of days."

"You got a camp up here?"

"Yep," I answered. "It's up the road a couple of miles."

"Have you seen anybody else up here the last few days?" asked the ranger.

"Nope, just Phil when he brought up some groceries a few days ago. Why do you ask?"

I had thoughts of bank robbers or modern

day thieves doing their crimes and hiding out in this wilderness area. It was really isolated.

"No particular reason," replied the ranger. "Hunting season is coming and I suspect some hunters might be in the area scouting for deer and elk."

"I've only seen a few elk since I've been here. A lot more deer."

"Well," said the ranger, "this area is closed to elk hunting. We want to build up the herd here. We transplanted some up here a few years ago. They seem to be doing okay, if we can keep the poachers out. If you see anybody or see some suspicious activity, make a note of it. Get license numbers and a description of the vehicles if possible. Then let us know."

I got kinda nervous when the ranger mentioned poachers. I was one of them! After all, I'd shot that deer out of season.

"How?" I asked. "I'll be up here a few more weeks an' there ain't no phone. I ain't figurin' on goin' to town until I'm done here."

"You get the information and give it to Phil when you see him. He can call it into the office. Then one of us will come out and check it out," replied the ranger.

He gave me his card, started the truck and

said, "We'll be seeing you more often. I expect to be up here checking out the country more often. Have a good day."

He drove off and I was glad I'd cooked up a lot of roasts and gave a quarter of the venison to Phil.

While scattering salt, I'd become a little familiar with the fence and the country. The first day fixing fence was fairly easy. I didn't come across any bad spots where the fence was down.

About mid-afternoon, I started back toward camp. I'd covered a lot of ground and figured I still had about four days of fence fixing ahead of me. When I arrived at camp, I was surprised to see the ranger's truck there. The ranger was laid out on the chaise lounge.

I tried to act as normal as possible, not letting any of the guilt about being a poacher show.

"You've got a pretty nice camp here," said the ranger. "A lounge chair and everything."

"This has been my home for the last couple of weeks," I said as I unsaddled One Spot, hobbled him, gave him some grain and turned him loose. "The lounge chair was somethin' one of Phil's friends threw in. You been waitin' here long?"

"Only about twenty minutes," answered the

ranger. "Not long enough to get a good nap. How's the fence?"

"So far, so good. Nothin' serious. Want somethin' to eat. All I got is canned beef stew, but you're welcome to it."

"No," replied the ranger. "I'll be home in time for supper. One thing I forgot to mention. The bow season opens up in a few days, then the muzzle-loading season, then the regular rifle season. Let me know if you see any four-wheelers up here. They can only stay on this road. We can't have them running all over the country, tearing up the ground."

"Sure," I said.

The ranger left and as I started supper, I had thoughts of being overrun by hunters and four-wheelers.

The next day I saddled Little Outlaw, replenished my supply of staples and clips and rode back to where I'd left off the day before. I expected Little Outlaw to act up as I fastened the clips to the steel posts and hammered in staples to the wood posts. But he didn't do anything after I'd done the first few.

When I arrived back at camp later that afternoon, I was surprised to see a motor home and a trailer with two four-wheelers on it parked about a hundred yards from my camp. There were some people gathered around the three horses I'd left at camp.

Somewhat disturbed that the serenity of my camp was being destroyed, I rode over to the invaders.

"What's goin' on here?" I asked.

There were two women and two men outside the motor home. The women were feeding the colts.

"We've come up here to hunt deer," answered one of the men. "We didn't think you'd mind if we camped here."

"What are you feedin' my horses?"

"It's just bread," answered one of the women.

"Don't feed 'em nothin'," I said, trying to be as stern as I could. I wanted to act as ornery as I could in an attempt to have them move their camp as far away as possible. "This is a private camp, set up here to keep track of cattle on this mountain."

"But this is such a pretty spot," said one of the women.

"There's another spot up the road a couple of miles. It's just as good as this one," I said.

"We'll move camp, if you wish," said one of the men.

"It might be best," I said.

I turned my horse to leave and while riding back to my camp, I imagined what the folks were saying about my lack of courtesy. They didn't seem too happy about moving camp. Before I left, I wrote down a description of the motor home and the license plate number.

I told Little Outlaw, "They're probably sayin' stuff like, 'He's an ignorant so-and-so,' or, 'who does he think he is, the owner?' Probably have a lot of cuss words about me!"

I got to my camp, unsaddled Little Outlaw, grained him and turned him loose. Then I got a bucket of grain and went after my other three colts. I grained them all and started my own supper. I heard the motor home start up and leave. I was relieved.

The next day I saddled Socks and started out to where I'd left the fence the day before. I headed up the road for a piece, just to see where the hunters had set up their camp. It was a little out of the way and when I saw it, I didn't ride into their camp. I noticed that they had an awning on the motor home and a couple of chaise lounges set up under it.

"Looks like I'm not the only one that enjoys all the comforts of home," I told Socks, as we left the road and started toward the fence. I smiled as I left.

Fixing fence that day was a little harder. There was one stretch, about a hundred yards long, where the fence was down completely. I got off Socks, hobbled him, and set about repairing fence. I wished I'd have brought the fence stretcher along, it would have made the job easier. But I improvised and where I needed extra barbed wire, I cut some from the bottom strand and used it where I needed it. In some places a five-wire strand of fence became a four-wire strand. Satisfied that I'd done as good as I could with what I had, I caught Socks, took the hobbles off, and continued on.

13

A few more days and I'd ridden the entire fence, fixing it as good as I could. I was content that it would hold the cattle in. I did see some elk higher up on the mountain. I also saw the hunters on their four-wheelers high up on the ridges.

One day when I returned to camp, I was surprised to see the ranger at camp. He was sprawled out on the chaise lounge again, taking a nap.

I unsaddled my horse, grained him, hobbled him, and turned him loose. The ranger woke up when I entered the tent.

"Howdy, cowboy," he said as I entered the tent.

"Howdy," I replied.

"Mighty comfortable camp you've got here!"

"Yep, it's home."

"Anything going on?" he asked.

"Not much, really. There's some hunters in

a motor home up the road a piece. They've got some four-wheelers an' been runnin' all over the country. I seen 'em up on the ridge a few days ago. Here's the license number," I said as I handed him the information I'd written down.

"Up on the ridge, huh?"

"Yep."

"I better check them out. They get anything yet?"

"I dunno. I ain't been to their camp. They originally set up camp not too far from here, but I run 'em off. I kinda like the solitude here."

"I don't blame you. I'll go visit with them. You have a good day."

The ranger left and I started fixing my supper.

About an hour later, the ranger returned.

"Those folks didn't have much good to say about you," said the ranger.

"They weren't too happy about movin' their camp," I said. "They get anything yet?"

"No. They said they'd just been scouting the area. I did give them a verbal warning about taking their four-wheelers off the road. They assured me that they hadn't."

"People do lie," I said.

"Now that we've got a few hunters in the area, I'll be back a little more frequently."

"Don't be surprised if I'm gone when you get here," I said. "I'm 'bout done here."

"You're not going to stick around and do some hunting?"

"Nope." My answer was short. I didn't want to tell the ranger I'd already got my deer. "I don't have a huntin' license," I added.

When Phil returned a few days later, we discussed how long I was to stay in camp.

"I thought I'd spend another week, then head to the ranch. It's startin' to get cold in the mornin's up here. What's the date anyways?"

"Tomorrow will be the tenth of October," said Phil.

"That late in the year? How time flies."

"Before you head to the ranch, open the gate where we let the cattle in last spring, then head home. The cattle will start heading down after the first snowfall. Don't worry about packing the tent and supplies. I'm thinking I'll come up here and use it during the rifle hunting season. There'll be a good home-cooked supper waiting for you when you get home."

"That sounds good to me," I said.

I spent the next few days checking cattle, then, on the last day, I went to the gate where we'd let the cattle onto the forest, opened the gate and tied it back against the fence. I was done and ready to go back to the ranch.

The next morning, I saddled Little Outlaw, put the pack saddle on One Spot, put my bed-roll on, haltered and tied the three colts together, and headed toward the ranch. I was kinda glad to be leaving. A storm was approaching from the west and it looked like snow. I didn't want to be on the mountain during a snowstorm.

At the ranch, I unsaddled the two horses, grained them all, took my bedroll to the bunk-house, went to my car and got some clean clothes. I took a long hot shower. I really enjoyed the shower. It was a lot better than bathing in the cold water in the creek.

During supper that night, Phil questioned me about my plans.

"I don't really have any plans," I said.

"We could sure use you about the middle of February when we start calving," said Phil.

"That's a long ways off," I said. "Too far for me to make plans for."

"You just keep it in mind. After breakfast in the morning, I'll have your check ready. You can cash it at the bank in town."

"Good," I said. "You sure you don't need any help bringin' the cattle home?" I asked. I didn't want to leave and have Phil shorthanded.

"Don't need any help," replied Phil. "The cattle will work down off the mountain when it gets cold."

THE END

Other Books by Stu Campbell

Horsing Around a Lot
Horsing Around the Dudes
Humor Around Horses
You Can't Be Serious!
Comedy Around the Corral
More Humor Around Horses
Muddy Waters
Comedy Around Cowboys
The Loner
The Drifter
The Life of a Cowboy
The Wagon

A Young Cowboy's Adventure Series

A Young Cowboy's Adventure
Honey
Surprise!
Intruders
Expectations
Frozen
Advice
Broken
Ginny

Wild Horses for Wild Kids
The Kids Get Horses

About the Author

Stu bases his books on his true-life experiences of ranch life and being a cowboy. He is a graduate of Utah State University with a degree in Animal Husbandry, and has also been a ski instructor, truck driver, and rancher.

About the Cover Artist

Cowboy artist, **R. Loren Schmidt**, is truly a cowboy and an artist. He illustrates from real life experiences from his lifetime of cowboying. A lifetime of dedicated art practice is evident in his expressive and accurate depictions of the contemporary cowboy experience. Loren is most inspired by his friends, horses, and the grand adventures in the backcountry of the West.